MISUNDERSTANDING THE BILLIONAIRE'S HEIR

A SWEET WATER HIGH ROMANCE

ANNE-MARIE MEYER

Sweet *Heart* Books

To My Uncle Jim

WELCOME TO THE TOWN OF SWEET
WATER, NC.

1 TOWN. 1 SCHOOL. 12 SWEET ROMANCES

CHAPTER ONE

"*Y*ou're crazy, you know that?" my best friend, Maddie, said as she slammed the register drawer closed and turned to stare at me.

"I'm not sure *crazy's* the right word." I tucked my red hair behind my ears and adjusted my black-rimmed glasses. "Smart was more what I was going for."

She shot me an exasperated look. "Charlotte, we're talking about Liam Johnson's party." She focused her bright, blue eyes on me and the intensity of her gaze caused me to twitch.

"I know," I said, as I reached out and fiddled with the stack of gift cards that were piled up on the counter. But that was the problem. I didn't fit in with her crowd. I never would. The sooner she realized it, the sooner we could go back to the way our friendship used to be. Before she got popular.

Besides, ever since my mom died last year, everyone was weird around me. Quiet and skittish. I didn't want to spend the whole night smiling at sympathetic gazes and pats on my shoulder.

The sound of the espresso machine filled the air. I glanced over and waited for Parker to finish what he was doing. Well, in all honesty, I was grateful for the break the noise gave me. It allowed me time to process how the heck I was going to get out of this party without telling her that I just didn't belong or want to go.

"I just...can't. I have to work and then it's my night to watch Drew. Dad's working tonight so I probably shouldn't go out." I gave her my best apologetic smile, hoping that it would appease her for now.

Maddie groaned and leaned both elbows on the counter. "It'll be fun." Then she stuck out her bottom lip. "Don't make me go alone. Please? Brody's going to be there and things are moving in the right direction with him." She wiggled her eyebrows.

Brody. Maddie's victim this week. She went through boys faster than a person with a box of tissues when they had a cold. I, on the other hand, had yet to even have a boyfriend. Or be kissed...

Why Maddie was my friend was beyond me. But, I guess a Kindergarten bond over mudpies was strong enough to keep us together.

Maddie sighed and blew a strand of highlighted blonde hair from her face. Her perfectly lined eyelids and dainty nose were definitely the reasons why every boy at Sweet Water High wanted to date her. Where she was tall and curvy, I was average height and thin.

Maddie drummed her fingers on the counter. "Fine. But you'll think about it, right?"

I chewed my lip and nodded.

"Are you just going to stand there all day or can other people order?" a strained voice asked from behind me.

Startled, I jumped to the side. When I turned to apologize, I saw a pair of dark brown eyes, perfectly formed lips, and a creased forehead. A guy I'd never seen before in my life was glaring at me.

I swallowed, muttered a small apology, and stepped out of the way.

"Lucas, be nice," a girl with long, wavy brown hair and the same deep brown eyes said as she walked up next to him and shot me an 'I'm sorry' look. She had a lace headband on and a flowy black dress that hit her mid-thigh.

I shook my head. "It was my fault."

"See, it's her fault," said the guy whom I could only assume was Lucas.

She shook her head. "Jacquline Addington. But you can call me Quinn," she said, extending her hand.

Lucas moved to order while I stood next to Quinn. She had a soft smile and unlike her brother, a kind look in her eye.

"What's your name?" Quinn asked me.

"Charlotte." I peeked over at her, trying not to stare. Sweet Water was a small town in North Carolina. Most people wore t-shirts or jeans. Sometimes, not even that. The beach was thirty minutes from where we stood and during the summertime, swimsuits and flip-flops were the norm.

Lucas and Quinn were too well dressed to be from around here.

Quinn didn't seem to notice my faded overalls and white t-shirt. If she did, she didn't seem to mind. Although, I made sure not to touch her. I had worked at the bakery this morning and didn't want to get any residual flour on her dress.

"Are you from around here?" I asked. I couldn't help myself. These two stuck out like a sore thumb and I had this strange desire to learn more about them.

Maddie finished taking Lucas' order and called, "Next!" Quinn shot me a sympathetic look and stepped up to order. I waited, not sure if we were continuing our conversation or if we were done.

Lucas had shoved his hands into his front pockets and was staring everywhere but at me. He had dark brown hair that was styled in a way that made it look like he wasn't trying—even though he so obviously was. His dark jeans were faded and ripped but I could tell they were made that way instead of worn from work.

"We just got here. We're from New York. Well..." She shot Lucas a look that was filled with...something. Regret? Understanding? Sympathy? Something.

"Why are you talking to her?" Lucas asked, turning to Parker who had just called his name. Quinn parted her lips to respond but Lucas just grabbed the coffee, mumbled something about heading outside to wait, and stomped out of the shop.

I couldn't help but glare at him. What was his problem? "Did they run out of coffee in New York?" I asked, turning my attention back to Quinn.

Her gaze lingered on the door as she sighed. "You'll have to excuse my brother. He's...going through something."

"You're related?" How can two people who were siblings act so different?

Quinn nodded. "Yeah. We're twins. He's not normally like this, I swear. He's just been struggling, you know?"

I scoffed. That was an understatement. We all go through things. I had had my share of *things* to go through. I swallowed as an all-too familiar pain rose up inside my gut. Tears stung my eyes. Why hadn't time healed the gaping wound inside my chest? A wound that could only have been formed by the loss of a parent.

Suddenly, I needed to get out of there. I needed the openness of the outside world. Not the cramped quarters of The Bean where the walls were slowly closing in on me.

"I've gotta go," I mumbled and headed to the door. Maddie called out something about talking to me later and I just waved my hand in her direction. I kept my gaze trained on the sidewalk as I hurried around the corner. Suddenly, I slammed right into what felt like a brick wall.

But brick walls didn't grunt or mutter stuff under their breath.

Not sure if I wanted to look up, I did anyway.

Lucas was staring down at me. His dark eyes were stormy and

hard. It took a few seconds for me to realize that I was wet…with steaming, hot liquid.

Finally, my brain registered that I'd had hot coffee dumped down the front of me. I yelped and began to attempt to wipe it off my skin.

"What's the matter with you?" Lucas asked, reaching over to a nearby table and grabbing a stack of napkins at the owner's protest.

I started to hold out my hand when I realized that he wasn't getting the napkins for me. Instead, he bent down and began to wipe the coffee off his tan loafers.

"These shoes are Italian," he said, like I should know where his footwear came from.

I stared at him, not sure what was going on. Thankfully, the liquid had cooled slightly in the ninety-degree summer heat. My skin no longer felt as if it were on fire. But that didn't excuse the fact that he was more worried about his shoes than the fact that I could have second degree burns on my chest.

"I'm fine," I snapped as I continued wiping the giant brown mess that was all over my clothes.

He glanced up at me and I wanted to punch him. There wasn't an ounce of sympathy or regret in his eyes. If anything, all I saw was annoyance.

"Well, you should watch where you're walking." He finished wiping his shoes, straightened, and just when I thought he was going to give me the rest of the napkins, he turned and flung them into the nearby garbage.

Red-hot fury coursed through me, rivaling the heat from his coffee. "What is the matter with *you?*" I asked, stomping over to the garbage and fishing out his discarded napkins.

He glanced into his cup and then chucked it into the garbage. It narrowly missed me and I had to jump out of the way to avoid any more coffee hurling my direction. This guy was a real piece of work.

"I'm going to get another cup of what this town calls coffee." He held my gaze for a moment before turning and heading back into the shop.

I glared at his back as hard as I could and dabbed my clothes with the napkins, and then dumped them back into the garbage. I was soaking wet and according to my watch, late for my second shift. I crossed Main Street and walked the three blocks to my house.

Dad was in the driveway underneath his "next big thing" as always. His feet stuck out and I could hear his drill, amongst his swearing.

Ever since Mom died, he'd thrown himself into his projects. Cars, motorcycles, snowmobiles. Anything he could find, he collected and stored in our yard, driveway, and backyard. We lived in a suburban junkyard.

Mrs. Protresca was standing in her yard, watering her petunias when I walked past her. She was staring at the large truck that had been parked right on the border where our properties met. I could see the frustration in her expression.

"Hey, Mrs. Protresca," I said, giving her the biggest smile I could.

Her gaze snapped to me. "What is this?" she asked, waving her hand to the towering monstrosity.

Frustration crept up inside of me. I told Dad we had to get rid of these vehicles, but he didn't listen to me. Something he was doing quite regularly lately.

"I know. I'm talking to him, Mrs. P."

Her expression softened for a moment before she got a determined look. "It's been a year, Charlotte. This can't keep happening. If your father doesn't clean up the yard, I'm going to have to complain to the city." She adjusted the readers that were perched on her nose and peered down at me.

I swallowed and nodded. "Of course. We'll get it cleaned up."

She gave me one more stern look before calling for her dog, Princess, and disappearing behind her house.

I sighed as I walked across the lawn and over to Dad. "Another one?" I asked.

Dad rolled out from under the car he was working on. "Hey, pumpkin." Then his gaze swept over me. "What happened to you?"

I waved his question away. He wasn't going to change the subject that fast. "What is this?" I moved my gaze to the car he was under. "You promised me there would be no more additions."

He pulled himself up to sitting and wiped his hands on a rag that had been threaded through his belt loop. "Yeah, but I got this one for a steal. Once I fix it up, we'll be able to sell it for triple what I paid for it." Then his gaze dropped to the front of my overalls. "Did you get any in your mouth?"

Realizing we weren't ever really going to have an open conversation about his need to salvage every vehicle that came across his path, I motioned toward my clothes. "A spoiled, rich kid spilled his coffee on me."

Dad's graying eyebrows went up. They matched his gray, thinning hair. Before Mom got sick, it had been dark and thick. But now? He looked old. He had dark circles under his eyes and always looked tired. I knew he was still hurting. We all were. But we couldn't get kicked out of our house. Not when this was the last place we'd lived with Mom.

Pain crushed my heart and I had to blink back my tears.

Dad must have seen my reaction because he cleared his throat, fiddled around with a few tools, and then laid back to roll under the car. "Don't forget, I've got to work tonight. You've got Drew."

Great. Typical Dad. Anytime anyone got sad, he shut down.

I wiped at my cheeks, angry with myself that I had allowed my emotions to get the better of me. I took in a few deep breaths and then turned toward the house. "I'll be home."

Once inside, I texted Winny to let her know I was going to be ten minutes late, took a quick shower, and dressed in a pair of cut off jeans and a tie-dyed tank. Once I had my shoes on, I was out the door and on my bike. I rode through the streets of Sweet Water taking note of all the familiar shops. The Bean was on the outskirts of downtown. Small shops lined the street and felt like home.

I waved and nodded to a few people who were either watering their flowers or sitting out with a newspaper and coffee. Just when I turned down Parsons Street, the familiar smell of The Bread Basket filled my nose and all the stress I'd been feeling rushed from my body.

This was where I belonged. Right now, this was the closest to a home I had. Here, life was simple. It was all recipes and baking. I didn't have to think. I could just create.

I skidded to a stop out back and climbed off my bike. After the kickstand was down, I turned and pulled open the back door. I paused just inside and grabbed my apron off its hook and strung it over my neck.

"I'm here, Winny," I called toward the kitchen. "I'm so sorry. I met this completely conceited guy at The Bean who spilled his coffee all over me so I had to go home and shower."

When she didn't answer, I finished tying the strings around my waist, and continued. She was probably elbow deep in dough.

"He was this awful out-of-towner. Acted like I was supposed to know that his shoes were *Italian*." I scoffed at the memory of Lucas bending down to wipe off his shoes. "I mean, a real jer—"

I rounded the corner and my words came to a screeching halt. Lucas was sitting on one of the bar stools next to the counter. Quinn was next to him, her lips pinched into a tight line, like she was trying hard not to laugh.

"Wha—what are you doing here?" I finally managed to say. This had to be a dream. Well, more like a nightmare. Why was he here looking all high and mighty? I had half a mind to walk over and give him a piece of my mind.

Winny appeared from the front. Her grey hair was pulled up

into a bun and her rainbow-colored spectacles hung from her neck. She had dark brown eyes that were warm and welcoming. "Oh, Charlotte, you're here." Then she paused as she studied my expression. "Everything okay?"

My brain didn't seem to want to work. All that was going through my mind on a repetitive loop was, *He's here* in neon letters. It must have shone on my face because she continued to stare at me with her eyebrows creased.

When I didn't answer, Winny glanced over to Quinn and Lucas and smiled. "Ah, so I see you've meet my grandkids."

CHAPTER TWO

I stared at Winny. What did she just say? "I'm sorry, your what?"

Winny gave me a confused look. "My grandkids."

Winny had family? "When did you get kids?"

A sad look passed over Winny's face as she cleared her throat and gave Lucas and Quinn a small smile. "I'm sure I've told you about my son."

I wanted to shake my head. I wanted to know how the heck this woman who was like a grandmother to me didn't tell me that she had a kid. I wanted to figure out how the nicest woman I knew could have such a spoiled and awful grandson. They were the complete opposite of each other. But, from the pleading look in her eyes to not push the matter, I just nodded. "Oh, right. I must have forgotten."

Lucas scoffed and pushed his hands through his hair. He looked uncomfortable and it made me smile. Good. He should feel uncomfortable. The way he treated me was unacceptable. That was not how a Sweet Water resident should behave.

Awkwardness filled the air as I moved my gaze from Winny

back to Lucas and Quinn. Finally, Winny turned around and gave me a smile.

She was fidgeting like she was nervous. It made me wonder what had happened with her son. "So what was your text about? Someone spilled their coffee on you?"

At the mention of the events earlier today, I snapped my attention over to Lucas who was studying the stainless steel countertop. "Yeah."

Winny shook her head. "Who was it?"

I sighed and gave her a small smile as I moved over to the flour container and pulled off the lid. "Just a nobody."

Quinn giggled and when Winny glanced over at her, she straightened her face.

"Well, I'm glad you're okay."

I shrugged. "I'm more than fine." And then I winced. There was nothing in that sentence, or the way I said it, that made me sound like I was more than fine. But I couldn't go back now so I just began measuring the flour and dumping it into the large mixer in the corner. "I'll get started on the dough for tomorrow."

Winny didn't seem to pick up on my awkwardness. Maybe it was because I already had it in spades. There was nothing about Charlotte Robinson that was smooth. People were probably used to me by now.

"Perfect. I'll bring Jacquline and Lucas upstairs and get Lucas settled, then I'll be back."

There was one word that stuck out to me and there was no way I was going to be able to survive the next ten minutes without asking. "Settled?"

Winny nodded as she motioned for Lucas and Quinn to follow. "That's right. Settled. He's staying with me for the school year."

I turned and closed my eyes. Just my luck. Lucas was staying here. With Winny. My safe haven was rapidly becoming my nightmare.

I took a deep breath as I began to fill a pitcher with water. I could do this. It wouldn't be that bad. I mean, maybe he was just crabby from his trip. Or the fact that he was relocating to a place he didn't know. I'm sure it had to be hard. I could give him the benefit of the doubt.

But as I watched the water dump over the flour, a sinking feeling formed in my gut. A familiar one that told me my initial evaluation of the situation was correct. This was going to be just as bad as I thought it was going to be.

Lucas was here to stay and unless I found a new job fast, I was going to have to see him regularly.

———

Thankfully, I had bread dough to keep me occupied. Once I forced out all those feelings of dread, I was able to relax. I was kneading dough on the counter when Quinn made her way downstairs from Winny's above-shop apartment.

I gave her a smile when she glanced over at me. I couldn't quite make her out. How could she be related to Mr. Snobby? She seemed so different.

"Hey, again," she said, settling in on the barstool that Lucas had vacated.

I nodded. "Hey."

She reached out and drummed her fingers on the counter. She glanced around, and I could tell something was up.

I was never good at lots of silence so I asked, "How long has it been since you've seen Winny, er—your grandmother?"

She glanced over at me. "Once, when I was eight. Dad's not too fond of her." Then she winced. "That was rude. What I'm trying to say is, they don't really get along."

I scoffed, finding that hard to believe. "Who couldn't get along with Winny?"

Quinn's phone chimed and she took a moment to check it before turning her attention back to me. "We kind of come from two different worlds."

"Yeah. I got that."

Quinn's forehead wrinkled as she studied me. Suddenly, I felt bad for what I had said. Quinn wasn't the rude one, Lucas was.

"I mean, you seem nice. Others seem more concerned about loafers than people." I hesitated, wishing I would just shut my mouth to stop the flow of words that seemed to be running from it.

Quinn studied me. "Lucas isn't all bad. He's just..." She reached out and fiddled with a measuring cup I'd left on the counter.

She kept doing this. Starting sentences and not finishing them when it came to her brother. Whatever it was that she was trying so hard not to say must be bad.

I shook my head, not wanting her to feel uncomfortable. "It's okay. I get it." I used my wrist to push up my glasses, which were sliding down my nose. "You don't need to explain your brother." I gave her a semi-confident smile. "I doubt we will even talk to each other again."

Quinn studied me and then nodded. She sighed and her phone chimed again. She glanced down and swiped at her screen.

I focused back on the dough, reveling in the feeling of the smooth material against my hands. There was so much that I loved about baking, but the biggest reason was that I had control. With baking, you knew that if you follow the recipe you will always get the same result. You'll end up with a fabulously delicious product in the end. Every time.

It was everything I needed in my life right now.

"So your friend Maddie is texting me," Quinn's voice broke through my thoughts.

I glanced over at her to see that she'd turned to study me. "Oh really?" That was strange.

She nodded. "Yep. Apparently, she wants us to go to a party tonight?"

I pinched my lips together. Maddie was relentless.

"Are you going?" Quinn's question threw me for a second.

I sighed as I shook my head. "I don't think so. I have to babysit my little brother and ever since my—" Nope. There was no way I was going to tell her about Mom. The more I talked about her, the more I breathed life into the pain that came every time I mentioned her name.

Keeping quiet seemed the best policy. I mean, that's why Dad did it. Right?

She seemed to be waiting for me to continue so I just rolled my shoulders and smiled at her. "And I'm tired."

She eyed me and I knew she didn't believe me, but she remained quiet so I returned to the dough.

Footsteps on the stairs drew my attention over. Winny and Lucas emerged from above. They both had strained expressions as they walked into the kitchen. I gave Winny a confused look but she just waved away my concern.

"Did you call your parents to let them know you got here safely?" Winny asked Quinn who nodded and explained that she texted her mom.

Lucas just moved toward the far wall where he leaned his shoulder against it. He got out his phone and stared at it. I couldn't help my gaze from drifting over to him every few seconds. Quinn and Winny seemed consumed with their conversation and as much as I was trying to ignore Lucas, I couldn't help but wonder what was going on with him.

Why would his parents ship him off to some small, unknown town? It was pretty obvious that he was rich. Why was he being banished here?

"Lucas, are you coming tonight?" Quinn's voice carried into my thoughts

Lucas snapped his gaze up and met mine. For a moment, I felt paralyzed. Why was I staring? I needed to stop. Right now. So I dropped my focus back down to the dough, hoping Lucas didn't notice that I'd been watching him.

"Go where?" he asked. From the corner of my eye, I saw that he'd moved his attention to Quinn.

"To the party at the beach."

He scoffed. "I'm sure it's not a party. More of a barn dance."

Heat pricked at my neck. Wow. If only it were socially acceptable to say the words that were threatening to spill from my lips. But I valued my self-respect, and my job, so I just chewed the inside of my cheek.

"It will be fun, Lucas. Besides, don't you want to get to know these kids before school starts?" My ears perked up at Winny's words.

So he was going to Sweet Water High. Maybe that was another reason for me to do post-secondary school at the Sweet Water Community College. A dream I'd had back when Mom was alive. Back when I didn't have to take care of Drew.

Sadness started to creep in, so I pushed out the thoughts of my future. I was such a fool to even allow myself to think that was a possibility anymore. Dad and Drew needed me. I couldn't go anywhere, and I wasn't sure I wanted to.

"I'm not staying that long. Dad will come to his senses and come back and get me." From the corner of my eye, I saw him shove his phone back into his pocket. "No need to make nice with locals."

His gaze landed on me, and my skin heated from the intensity it held. Out of self-preservation, I kept my focus ahead.

"Wes will be there," Quinn said.

That seemed to get Lucas thinking but then he shrugged. "Nah. I'll just hang out here."

Whoa. Maybe I should be pushing him to go. There was no

way I wanted him to be here, stuck with me. "You should go. It'll be fun. Liam always throws the best parties. They are amazing." I tried to keep my voice as sweet as honey and gave him my best *you know you want this* smile.

Lucas furrowed his brow as he studied me. I held my smile even though all I wanted to do was return his scowl.

"See, even Charlotte thinks this is a good idea." Quinn's words sounded just as sweet as mine.

"She does? Sounds to me like she wants to get rid of me." He shot me a look, but I held my ground.

"Of course she doesn't want to get rid of you. She's actually coming with."

I snapped my gaze over to Quinn. What was she doing? I already told her that I couldn't go. "I'm not—"

"I can watch Drew," Winny offered.

I moved my attention over to her. "What? How did you know—?"

"Your Dad called when I was upstairs to see if Drew could come over here. Apparently he has a lead in Buxton County and can't take him with. I told him that was fine."

My stomach plummeted to the floor. Dad was off to get another find? What was he doing to us? I shook my head. None of that mattered right now. Not when my life was getting planned for me. I put on the best apologetic smile I could muster. "I really should stay with Drew." I shrugged and started separating out the dough, trying to end this conversation.

"Nonsense. You should go. You work too hard. Besides, you would be doing me a favor, helping Lucas fit in."

Lucas scoffed, but I ignored him. Instead, I glanced up to see Winny's earnest face. She looked lost and maybe a little hurt. And underneath it all, she looked hopeful.

Ugh. There was no way I was going to be able to say no to that. I inwardly groaned as I nodded.

"Fine."

Quinn squealed and leapt off her stool. "This will be so much fun," she said, rushing over to throw her arms around me and give me a squeeze.

"Yeah," I whispered as she let go of me to hug Lucas. "Fun."

Except fun was the last word I would use to describe this.

CHAPTER THREE

"*D*rew, stop bouncing on Winny's bed," I scolded my brother as I reached out to grab his arm. He saw me coming and ducked so that I ended up just flopping down onto her comforter.

I let out an exasperated sigh as I flipped to my back. "You're a brat."

He stopped bouncing so he could peer over me. His glasses sat crooked on his nose and his big grin showed his missing teeth. "Dad said you can't call me that anymore."

I glared at him and then reached up and took a hold of his arms. He struggled but I managed to get him down and started to tickle him. He squealed and struggled, but it didn't matter. I was still a bit stronger than him. Which wouldn't last forever. He was ten and almost as tall as me.

"Lottie, no!" he screamed as I kept tickling him.

Movement next to me drew my attention over and in an instant I stopped tickling Drew. Lucas was standing in the doorway, studying us. His arms were folded, and he was leaning against the frame. I cleared my throat and stood up, patting down my hair as I was sure it was sticking up everywhere.

Lucas quirked an eyebrow as he kept his gaze on me.

What was with him? Why was he just standing there, staring at me? It was so...so...exposing. Like he could see into my soul or something. It definitely made me uncomfortable.

"Can we help you?" I asked, placing my hands on my hips. Then, feeling like a dork, I dropped them to my side and then folded them across my chest. Great. Now I was fidgeting like an idiot.

Drew didn't seem to notice the tension in the air. Instead, he was back up and bouncing away. I glared at my brother and I must have gotten through to him because he finally settled down, snuggling into Winny's comforter.

"Just wondering if you were ready to go," Lucas asked, with his gaze never leaving my face.

I patted my hair down again. His stare was unnerving me. And for some reason, I'd convinced myself that the only reason someone would stare at me like Lucas was staring at me was because my hair looked psychotic. Or I had food on my face...or worse. Maybe I should excuse myself and go to the bathroom.

But then, that would mean that I cared what Lucas thought about me. Which I didn't. So I kept my arms folded and held my ground. "Yes, I'm ready."

"No, you're not." Quinn appeared next to Lucas. She had changed into a crop top with frayed shorts. She, of course, looked like a Greek goddess with her long brown hair flowing around her.

It was almost comical how picturesque she looked.

"I'm not?" I asked, glanced down at my clothes.

She shook her head. "You're not going to a party in that." She waved at me.

"I'm not?" I repeated, pulling at my shirt.

She scoffed. "Now that we are friends, I'm going to help you." She pushed past Lucas and walked over to me where we linked arms.

After a soft tug, I obeyed as I followed her out of the room. I glanced back at Drew who had pulled out his iPad and was starting it up.

As we passed Lucas, I heard him chuckle softly and I thought I heard him say "Good luck" but when I glanced over at him, he had his lips shut.

Must have been my imagination.

Quinn pushed me into the only other bedroom in Winny's tiny apartment. All of Winny's paints and brushes were pushed to the side and a small twin bed sat along the far wall. There was a dresser and a nightstand and that was it.

A large suitcase sat propped open on the bed. Quinn headed over to it and started pulling out clothes.

I watched her as she took out as many clothes as would have constituted most of my wardrobe and stacked them next to the suitcase.

"I'm confused, are you staying in Sweet Water too?" I stepped up to her and glanced inside of the luggage. She'd only taken out half the items.

She laughed. "No. Just Lucas. I'm heading back home tomorrow. School starts soon."

I glanced over at her. "In New York?"

She nodded. "It's a prep school."

"Wow." I really didn't know much about prep schools beside the fact that you wore a uniform and paid a lot of money to go there.

Those thoughts made me wonder, just how rich were they? From the way Winny lived, I would have never expected that she came from money.

I wasn't sure how to tactfully ask, 'so, how rich are you?' Instead, I decided on a more scenic route. "Are the public schools in New York that bad?"

Quinn glanced over at me. "No, not really." She shrugged as she pulled out a fitted black mini-dress. I raised my eyebrows, hoping she would pick up on the fact that there was no way I was going to wear an outfit that small.

"My dad owns an investment company. I think he would die if I went to public school or even dated a guy from public school." Her expression softened. The way she said it made it seem like there was a guy from public school that she wanted.

Hmm...

A few seconds later, she snapped her attention over to me and gave me a smile. "Wow. Sorry. Didn't mean to do that." She pulled a dark blue, short romper and handed it over.

I studied it. Sure, it wasn't something I would pick out, but I didn't hate it. And she looked so earnest that I felt bad about complaining.

Quinn turned around and I slipped into the romper. Once I had it on, I told her she could turn around. Then she ushered me over to the chair where she put some mascara and lip-gloss on me and fiddled with my hair.

She declared me finished and ushered me out, saying we were going to be late. I wanted to protest. To tell her that I wanted to make sure she did a good job—that I didn't look like a clown—but she didn't listen.

Instead, I found myself descending the stairs right when Lucas appeared. He stood at the bottom, staring at his watch.

"Take long enough?" he asked and when he raised his gaze to meet mine, a look passed over his expression that made my heart pound just a bit harder.

I swallowed, cursing myself for letting that happen. He was a jerk. There should be no reason why my body was reacting to him at all. I gave him a smug look as I took the last step and found myself a foot away from him.

"Sorry we took so long," I said.

He flexed his jaw and swallowed so hard that I could see his muscles twitch. He gave me one last look before turning his focus on Quinn. "If you're dragging me along you might try to be on time."

Wow. He really was something. I gave him my most menacing stare, but if he noticed, he didn't move to show he cared.

Quinn didn't seem phased by his words. Instead, she rolled her eyes and pulled open the door. "Come on, Mr. Grumpy Pants," she said, shooting him a sarcastic smile.

I grabbed my flip-flops and purse, called a goodbye to Drew and Winny, and then ducked out after them. They walked over to a sleek, black car parked out front of the bakery. It definitely did not look like it fit in Sweet Water.

"Nice car," I said as I pulled open the back door and slipped onto the supple leather seats.

Quinn shot me a smile. "Thanks. It's a rental."

I nodded. "Well, it's nice." Then my gaze made its way over to Lucas who was buckling in the passenger seat. Did he have a car this fancy? From what Quinn said, I half expected him to have a limo.

"Lucas got his car taken away," Quinn said as if she'd read my thoughts.

Lucas shot her an annoyed look.

Quinn shrugged. "What? It's true. It's not like she's not going to figure that out."

"Quinn." Lucas's eyes narrowed as he stared at his sister.

Sensing a family fight coming on, I raised my hands. "It's okay. I don't need to know." In fact, the less I knew about Lucas, the better. I had no intention of being his friend or even his acquaintance. I was going to this party tonight to introduce him to some people and then I was cutting him from my life.

I didn't need another thing, or person, to worry about. My head was already swimming from the pain and responsibility I felt with Mom being gone, I didn't need a spoiled brat on my conscience as well.

The atmosphere in the car grew quiet. I sat back, trying to

relax against the tension around us. Something had happened. I could only imagine what it was. Maybe Lucas crashed his family yacht. Or destroyed some expensive family heirloom.

I mean, isn't that what most party boys do? Take and destroy without any thought for the person they were hurting? Just from looking at Lucas, I could tell he thought little about other people. He was so wrapped up inside of himself that he could literally spill coffee on someone and not care about how they felt.

Such a typical rich kid.

Quinn's phone announced we'd arrived at our destination. She pulled into the parking lot that lined the beach. In the distance, I could see the glow of the bonfire and hear the thumping of the music. After she shut off the car, we opened our doors and stepped out.

Quinn waited for me and then we linked arms. Lucas didn't wait for anyone. Instead, he made his was over to the bonfire without even looking back. I glared at his retreating frame. What was with him?

"Don't mind my brother," Quinn said.

I turned to see her watching me. I wanted to know what had happened. Why had her parents decided to dump him on us instead of dealing with whatever he'd done? Was it weird to inquire?

"He's really not happy being here," I said.

Quinn nodded. "That's an understatement."

I chuckled. We stepped onto the fine white sand of the beach. The grains squished between my toes and I instantly relaxed. There was something about the ocean that calmed me. Maybe it was the sound of the waves or the smell of salt, but it reminded me of my mom and a time in my life when I was actually happy.

Sadness tugged at my heart and for a moment, I closed my eyes. Mom. I could still see her smile and the way her eyes crinkled at the sides when she laughed.

"You okay?" Quinn asked, snapping me from my reverie.

I glanced over at her and nodded. "What? Um, yep."

She squeezed my arm. "Good. I'm so happy we met."

I nodded as we walked up to the group that was swarming the snack table.

"You came!" Maddie's voice cut through the music. She rushed over and wrapped her arms around me. "Oh my gosh. You look amazing," she said, pulling back and sweeping her gaze over me.

I blushed, hating the praise she was giving me. I liked keeping to the shadows where no one noticed me. Having half the school staring at me because Maddie's voice was as loud as a blow horn was not something I wanted. I grabbed her arm and pulled her to the side.

"Can you keep it down?"

She grinned at me. "So the rich hottie is here."

Wow. She could jump topics faster than a cockroach could run. "What?"

Her gaze drifted over to where Lucas was standing. He was talking to Wes Schultz, the star cross-country runner and rich kid of Sweet Water. Of course. Birds of a feather.

"You're welcome," she said.

"Wait. You invited him here for me?"

She chewed her lip and nodded. "Well, for you. For me. I'm not picky."

I laughed and raised my hands. "You can have him. I don't want him." Then I furrowed my brow. "What about Brody?"

Maddie sighed as she flicked her hair over her shoulder. "He's taking too long."

I rolled my eyes. "Which is Maddie lingo for *you got bored with him.*"

She dropped her jaw. "I did not."

I snorted. "Right." I reached out and patted her shoulder. "Well, you have my blessing to go after Lucas. There is no way on God's green earth that I want anything to do with him. Ever."

CHAPTER FOUR

$\mathcal{T}$he next hour played out just as I thought it would. Maddie flirted with every guy that crossed her path. Even Quinn was distracted with a plethora of Sweet Water guys. But me? I seemed to be invisible. I was either bumped into or the recipient of sloshed drinks across my feet when people stumbled.

I winced as yet another student plowed into me. Cold, wet liquid sloshed on my arm, drawing my attention to the perpetrator. He was tall, built and someone I didn't recognize.

"Sorry," he mumbled. He reached out to wipe off my arm but I pulled it back. He flicked his gaze over to me.

"It's okay. I've got it," I said.

He studied me before nodding and joining the rest of the football players. I wiped my skin and then shook my hand off, but nothing would take the sticky feeling away.

"I see you met Jason Hunt," Maddie's voice drew my attention over to her.

"Jason?"

She nodded. "Yeah. He's new. Just moved here. Apparently, a godsend for the football team."

I glanced at him and studied his build. "Well, he looks

menacing enough." I sighed and opened and closed my hand, hating the feeling of my skin sticking together.

Maddie slipped her arm through mine, linking us together. "Are you not having fun?"

I forced a smile. "Of course I am. Why would you say that?"

Maddie giggled and leaned in. "You look like you have a stick up your…" She nodded toward my behind.

Annoyed, I pushed away from her. "Gee, thanks. And you're wondering why I'm not having a good time."

Maddie held up her hands. "Hey, I'm just saying."

I shot her a look. "I'm going to rinse off my hand in the ocean."

She saluted me and then wandered off to flirt with some guy I couldn't make out.

Finally alone, I walked toward the ocean. Toward the water. The sound of lapping waves filled my ears. I took a deep breath, letting the scent of the sea wash over me.

I waded into the water until it covered my feet and then I began to walk down the shore. The sound of the party grew fainter the farther I walked.

My shoulders began to relax. My muscles loosened. I glanced out at the water and the itch to swim took over me. I'm not a fast swimmer. In fact, Mrs. Borton was what one would classify as kind to even let me stay on the team. But she had been friends with my mom, and what had once been a favor had turned into an act of sympathy.

I wasn't the worst, but I most certainly wasn't the best.

But right now, none of that mattered. I wanted to swim.

Glancing around, I made sure I was alone. There was a life-guard tower to the left but other than that, I'd gone far enough from the view of the party. The darkness of the sky around me helped me feel protected. And right now, I needed that.

I slipped off the romper until I was standing in my underwear and bra. The warm breeze cooled my skin, causing goosebumps to rise up all over my body. I felt a little dangerous, swimming in the ocean alone. I mean, ever since Mom died, I'd been really careful with the activities I did. But tonight, it felt so freeing to do something out of the norm.

Before I convinced myself to stop, I took a deep breath and ran into the water, letting it cover my body as I dove inside.

My body shifted in the waves as they beat against the shore. It wasn't until I was a good fifty feet out that the water stilled.

I surfaced to take a deep breath, and then allowed my body to sink into the water. It was peaceful here. Calm and serene. Here, there was no loss. Here, it was just me.

I let my breath leave my lips and felt it bubble up around me. My lungs ached, needing air, but I stayed under the water. I guess it was a reminder that I was alive even though Mom wasn't. Pain signified that I was here without her.

Just before I thought my body would burst from the need of air, I splashed to the surface, took another deep breath, and slipped back under the water. It was strange, but I felt close to Mom when I was under the water. It was the only place where I felt calm. The bakery used to give me that same feeling, but with Lucas here, I doubted that I would feel that way again.

If only I could stay here forever, the ache in my chest just might disappear. I might disappear.

I began to move to the surface again when two very strong hands grabbed onto me and pulled up hard. Startled, I gasped, taking in a mouthful of water. When I broke the surface, I coughed and sputtered, trying to make sense of what was happening.

Who had me and why were they dragging me to the shore?

Every time I cleared my throat, I opened my lips to speak only to have the water suffocate my words. I could feel my supposed rescuer place their feet on the ground and in a swift movement, pulled me up to cradle me.

I blinked a few times until my eyes focused, then all feeling left my body.

Lucas was carrying me to shore.

I was too stunned to speak. What was happening?

Once he cleared the water, he laid me down on the sand and disappeared for a moment.

It must have been the fact that I had taken in what felt like a gallon of ocean water, because my body wasn't working. I tried to force myself to sit up. To move my arms and legs and get as far away from Lucas as I could, but no amount of mental screaming at my body to work got me to move.

Lucas appeared in my line of sight. He studied my face then dipped down to feel if I was breathing—or that's what I thought he was doing. I really couldn't tell what his objective was. The only thing going through my mind was, if I didn't say anything very soon, my first kiss would be a strange attempt to save my life.

"I'm fine," I managed to yell and then heat flushed my body at the decibel to which it came out met my ears.

Lucas' gaze snapped to me and I took in a deep breath to speak, which threw me into a coughing fit. Not wanting to lay in the sand anymore, I shifted to sit but was having a hard time. Lucas reached out and grabbed onto my hand and shoulder to help me up. For some ridiculous reason, my skin heated from his touch.

I cursed my out-of-control reaction.

When my coughing subsided, I glared at him. "What was that?"

He remained kneeling by my side. Water glistened across his ridiculously tanned and, of course, ripped chest. Why did someone so rude have to reside in someone so...hot? I blinked a few times, forcing those thoughts from my mind.

"I thought you were drowning," he said.

I coughed a few times and when I glanced down, I suddenly remember that I was in my underwear. And I was wet. Trying to cover every part of me that I could, I wrapped my arms around my stomach and brought my knees up.

"I wasn't drowning. I was swimming." Then realization

dawned on me. "Did you follow me?" Heat raced across my skin. "And watch me undress?"

A small smile played on his lips as his gaze dropped to the ground. His reaction angered me so much.

"I didn't follow you, you followed me. And I didn't watch you undress. I was about to stop you when you took off your clothes. I thought I'd save you the embarrassment and just went to the other side of the beam." He nodded toward the lifeguard tower behind us.

I shivered. It wasn't from the temperature but from how exposed I felt.

Lucas stood and walked a few feet over to his clothes. It was only then when I realized that he was in his boxers. My heart pounded so hard I thought it was going to explode in my chest.

What was happening to me?

Lucas returned with his clothes. He handed me his t-shirt. I hesitated before taking it from him.

"Thanks," I muttered, as I slipped it on.

Lucas nodded, shook out his pants and then stepped into them.

Feeling so confused, I sat there, not sure what I was supposed to do. Did I thank him? It felt rude not to. But he didn't save me— he almost drowned me.

Man, my thoughts were so mixed up right now.

"I wasn't drowning," I said, giving up on thinking and reaching out to trace circles in the sand.

He glanced over at me. "You were under the water for a long time and when you came up, you were like, thrashing."

I looked up at him. "I'm a swimmer. I can swim. I'm on the swim team."

Gah, stop saying swim.

I pinched my lips together. Maybe it was best if I didn't talk.

Lucas rubbed his hands through his hair spraying ocean water everywhere. His expression was a pained one. I hoped I hadn't embarrassed him. I mean, if I really had been drowning, I'd want him there, saving me.

"Sorry. I guess old habits die hard." His attempted smile just looked like a grimace.

I tried to dissect what he was saying. Old habits? "Have you made it a habit to save girls from the ocean?" I hoped the teasing in my voice would help lighten the mood.

He turned to focus out on the water. "I, um..." He talked so quietly that the wind whisked his words away before I could hear them.

I leaned in, hoping to catch the end to that sentence, but I heard nothing. Huh. He must not have finished what he was saying.

Instead, he cleared his throat and motioned toward the party. "I'm going to go back."

I stared at his broad shoulders and ridiculously sculpted abs. I mean, Greek Gods would be jealous. "Are you—are you sure when you, you know..." I waved at him.

His gaze followed my motion and stopped on his chest. Then he glanced back up at me and there was an emerging half smile playing on his lips. Heat burned my cheeks as I dropped my gaze to study the sand. He knew I had noticed. Great.

"I think I'll be okay. It is the beach after all."

I nodded, chewing my lip. I wanted to keep my mouth busy so I didn't keep saying all the stupid things that came to my mind.

From the corner of my eye I saw him pass by me. My shoulders relaxed when he disappeared from view. Just as I brought my gaze up to study the ocean, he stepped back into view causing me to yelp.

"Charlotte?"

"Yeah. Uh huh?" My name sounded strange on his lips and threw me off guard. Was it wrong that I...liked it?

"Don't go into the ocean unless someone is around, okay?"

I stared at him. I wanted to say that I was a swimmer and that I hadn't been drowning, but I think I had established that earlier. So I just pinched my lips together and nodded.

He focused his attention on me for a moment longer before he turned and headed in the direction of the party.

Now alone, I laid back on the sand, staring up at the sky. The stars were bright and twinkling. I took a deep breath as I tried to calm my nerves. Every point of contact where Lucas had touched me was still tingling.

What had that been?

From the way he treated me earlier, you would have thought I had a fungus all over my skin. Now, he was saving me? Sharing his shirt with me?

I felt the fabric with my fingers. The cotton he got from his expensive stores must be grown somewhere else than the shirts I had. It was softer and smelled—I took in a deep breath—like spices and vanilla. I could breathe that scent all day long.

And then I felt like a dork. Here I was, lying on the beach, smelling Lucas' shirt.

When had things come to this?

I waited a few minutes before pulling myself to stand and walking over to my romper where I slipped it on under Lucas' shirt. My underwear was still wet, but not sopping like it had been when I got out of the ocean.

I grabbed my shoes and headed back to the party.

Maddie's eyes widened when she saw me. Her jaw dropped in an exaggerated movement. I couldn't help but roll my eyes at her reaction.

"What happened to you?" And then she leaned in and wiggled her eyebrows. "And why are you wearing Lucas' shirt."

This had been one colossal mistake. Why had I even come here?

At home I was safe. Here, I wasn't. Now more than ever since Lucas came to town.

"I went for a swim and Lucas thought I was drowning so he

ran into the water to save me." The truth seemed like the best route to go.

Maddie got a sinister look in her eyes. "Right," she said, dragging out the word.

I gave her an exasperated look. "It's true. Nothing happened."

She turned and out of instinct, I followed her gaze. Lucas was standing on the other side of the fire, talking to Wes. My heart hammered in my chest at the memory of him wrapping me up in his arms. How I felt as if I weighed nothing as he carried me.

"You're telling me, there's nothing going on there?" Maddie glanced back at me. The look in her eye told me, the only way a girl would be around a guy like that and not feel things would be if she was crazy—or blind.

"I'm telling you, Lucas is a jerk. I have no interest in him like that." I held my ground even though I could feel the walls of my resolve crumbling around me.

Lucas was a jerk. A guy who spilled his coffee on me and then acted like I didn't matter. His family didn't even like him. Why else would they banish him to Sweet Water?

No. It didn't matter that he'd just attempted to save my life. It didn't matter that his ridiculous half-smile made my insides turn to mush.

Lucas Addington was never going to be more than a selfish, super-hot, imposter. Ever.

CHAPTER FIVE

*T*he next morning, my alarm went off too soon. I groaned as I reached over to my nightstand and grabbed my phone.

3:30am

I squinted at the time, cursing myself for agreeing to work the morning shift. I'd offered to do it to pay Winny back for watching Drew. She said it hadn't been a problem, but I had insisted.

I was stupid.

I closed my eyes and moments later, my phone chimed. Knowing I'd fall asleep again if I didn't get up right now, I flung my covers off my body and forced myself to stand.

After I showered and dressed, I felt a bit better. I pulled my wet hair up into a messy bun and slipped my glasses on before grabbing my phone and heading downstairs.

Since I was headed to a bakery, I didn't bother to grab any breakfast. Instead, I wrote a quick note for Dad and then headed outside to get my bike.

Downtown was eerily quiet as I peddled down the road. The sun was still hidden behind the horizon, but its glow was starting to light up the sky. In the morning, there was a clean, fresh feel outside. I could smell the hint of salt from the ocean and feel the morning breeze on my face. It surrounded me with peace and for the first time in a long time, the stress that normally bore down on me lessened.

It didn't take long before I leaned my bike on its kickstand and pulled open the back door of The Bread Basket. I slipped inside and grabbed my apron before making my way into the kitchen.

Neil, the only other baker who worked for Winny, was bobbing his head up and down as he pulled a tray of rolls from the oven.

"Hey," I said as I walked over to the sink and began to wash my hands.

When Neil didn't respond, I looked closer and saw that he had earbuds in. After I dried my hands, Neil turned and jumped. He pulled his earbuds from his ears.

"You scared me," he said, holding his heart.

I laughed. "I did say hey."

He strung the cord around his neck. "I didn't hear you."

I shrugged and moved to the counter where the list that Winny had made was laying. "This the list?"

Neil nodded. "Yep. I'm working on the dinner rolls right now if you want to start the cinnamon bread."

I wasn't going to argue with that. Cinnamon bread was my favorite. I made my way to the fridge where I found the dough that I had made up the day before. After pulling it out and warming it in the proofer, I floured the countertop and plopped the dough on it.

After working it with my hands a few times, I rolled it out into a rectangle. Then I buttered it and sprinkled it with cinnamon sugar.

Neil and I worked until 5. After he pulled the last multigrain loaf from the oven, he dusted his hands off and shot me a smile.

"I gotta go. You're good with taking over?"

Too distracted by creating cinnamon rolls with perfect spirals, I nodded without looking up. "I'm good."

He washed his hands and took off his apron. The sound of the back door closing filled the air.

I took a deep breath and glanced around, the feeling of complete satisfaction filling my chest. This was where I belonged. Here, I was safe. I grabbed my phone and turned on an eighties music station.

I hummed along with the lyrics and I busied myself finishing up the cinnamon rolls and started the doughnuts. Sweet Water's pride and joy. Every baking competition this city held ended with Winny in first place for her delicious doughnut creations.

I had two hours before people would be pounding down her door for them. I needed to get started before I had a riot on my hands.

I cleaned my station after I slipped the last pan of cinnamon rolls into the oven. Thankfully, Neil started the doughnut dough when he got here because it was perfectly raised when I grabbed it.

"I didn't take you for an eighties music fan," Lucas' deep voice startled me, causing me to yelp and turn so fast that the bowl of dough slipped from my fingertips.

It was like slow motion, watching the bowl fall toward the floor. My mind couldn't quite get my hands to grab it even though I was screaming at them to move faster.

Lucas appeared in my line of sight and had the bowl in his grasp seconds before it hit the floor.

My heart pounded as he straightened and set it on the counter and then turned to me, a sheepish look on his face.

"I'm, um, sorry. I didn't mean to startle you."

My lips were parted and there was a ringing in my ear as my body tried to process what had almost happened. I didn't know what Winny would have done if I had finished this morning with no doughnuts.

"Th-thanks," I said, leaning against the cupboard as I tried to get my body to return to equilibrium.

Lucas glanced over at me and for a moment, I thought I saw a genuine smile tease at the corner of his lips. But as quickly as it came, it was over and he was back to his regular scowl.

"Your music woke me up," he said, running his hands through his damp hair.

Man, he looked great in the morning. Unlike me. I was covered in flour and bits of dough. He was wearing what I could only assume were designer jeans and a light blue button up shirt that looked both expensive and casual at the same time.

And, of course, the color of his shirt highlighted his skin, deepening his tan and making his brown eyes stand out. It was a crime that he looked this good when his personality stunk as bad as it did.

Not sure what I should say to his statement, I mumbled a sorry and watched as he walked over to the coffee machine and poured a mug.

I thought maybe he'd leave me alone after he got his caffeine fix, but instead of walking out the door, he just turned and leaned against the counter behind him. I tried to busy myself with the dough as I pulled it from the bowl and rolled it out onto the counter.

Heat pricked at the back of my neck and flushed my skin as his gaze stayed trained on me.

Why was he staring at me? Why hadn't he left? If I was such a terrible person to him, why was he sticking around?

After I'd cut out all the doughnuts, I brought them over to the fryer. I could feel him watching me as I moved across the room. It irritated me. I wanted to ask him what his problem was. Why he was nice to me and then so...rude.

"What are your plans today?" I asked. I decided not to let him bother me anymore. If he was going to stay in the kitchen, he was going to talk to me.

When he didn't answer, I glanced behind me as I slipped the dough into the fryer. I winced as one plopped in a bit too hard and splashed hot oil onto my arm.

"What is there to do in a town like Sweet Water?" The tone is his voice made me want to punch him. Like our small, quaint town wasn't good enough for the likes of him.

"A lot. If you're not pretentious and spoiled." I pinched my lips as the last words left my lips. I hadn't meant to say that much or to say them in that way. Just because he was rude, didn't mean I had to be. I could rise above that.

Not sure how to redeem myself, I returned my focus to the fryer and flipped the doughnuts over so they could brown on the other side.

"Do you not like me?" he asked.

My shoulders tightened at his question. How was I supposed to answer that? My first inclination was to say, no. But I wasn't too proud of what I had said earlier when I didn't filter my mouth. So I decided to take a moment to think through my response.

"I don't know you." Hmmm, that was good. Vague. Non-specific. And the truth. There was very little that I knew about him.

From the corner of my eye, I saw him set his mug down on the counter and then turn to fold his arms across his chest. "What do you want to know?"

A scoff escaped my lips. Was he for real? Was he going to answer the questions that had been buzzing in my head since the moment I saw him at The Bean?

Okay. If he was willing to be honest, I'd take him up on that.

"Why did you act like you didn't care that you spilled coffee on me?" After pulling out all the doughnuts, I turned to face him. To make sure he didn't weasel out of his offer to have a conversation with me.

His lips tipped up into a smile, which really irked me—and maybe made him a tad bit cuter. But only a tad.

"I'm sorry. I should have worried about spilling my coffee on you." He sighed and straightened, pushing his hands through his hair. "I just, had a lot on my mind." He took a few steps closer to me, and my heart instantly picked up speed.

I cleared my throat, refusing to let his proximity confuse me. "That's no excuse. We all have a lot on our minds. That doesn't mean we can be rude to people."

He nodded as he inched closer to me. "Are you ever going to forgive me?"

He was about a foot away from me, staring me down.

My emotions began to swirl. I could smell his cologne and feel his presence. Even though he wasn't touching me, I was still very aware of how close he was standing.

Forcing myself to gather my strength and not let his ridiculous...whatever it was, confuse me, I raised my eyes and held my ground.

"You never asked for forgiveness."

A half-smile emerged on his lips bringing heat racing across my body and settling on my cheeks.

Could he see it? Did he know what it meant? Because I didn't. Right now, it went against everything I was forcing myself to think about Lucas.

He leaned closer. "Will you forgive me?"

My eyes involuntarily dropped to his lips and for the second time, I notice how perfectly formed they were. Like, I was pretty sure artists spent their entire lives trying to recreate that type of perfection. "I—um..." *Speak, Charlotte!*

He inched closer. So close, that I was pretty sure he *was* going to kiss me. Did I want him to? I was so confused I didn't even know how to answer that.

"I guess," I whispered and felt myself lean into him.

Out of the corner of my eye, I saw him reach out and suddenly, a doughnut was in his mouth and he was pulling away. He winked at me as he pulled the doughnut from his lips and began chewing. "Great. I'm glad we got that out of the way."

I stood there, dumbfounded as he walked over to his coffee, grabbed it and then made his way to the stairs. When he got halfway up, he stopped and turned around.

"These were a little too brown. You might want to watch that. Don't want to ruin the Addington name with overcooked doughnuts." He shoved the rest of the doughnut into his mouth and disappeared upstairs.

As soon as he was gone, reality came crashing down around me. Irritation and anger brewed inside me as I glared at the stairs. What a jerk. He manipulated me into forgiving him. Manipulated me into almost kissing him. What the heck had I been thinking?

On top of it all, I seriously doubted he even felt sorry for what he did. Now, instead of having something over him, I just handed the ball back to his court. He got out of literally dumping hot coffee all over me, and I let him.

What a stupid thing for me to do.

And not only that, he had insulted my doughnut making skills.

I glowered at the dough as I began slipping them into the oil. I'd show him. I was going to make *the* best doughnuts the town of Sweet Water had ever had.

And then, I was going to find a way to get back at that spoiled, rich, new kid who seemed to think that this town was beneath him.

A slow, maniacal smile spread across my lips. This was going to be good.

CHAPTER SIX

*L*ater that afternoon, I sat in the rotunda of Sweet Water's mall, sipping on a tropical smoothie. My plan to make *the* best doughnuts Sweet Water had ever had was a success. I was literally glowing from the praise that everyone gave me.

Even Winny commented on how delicious they were. And she did it right in front of Lucas.

Score one for me.

I couldn't help the smug smile I gave him as he stood behind her with his eyebrows raised. I waited for him to comment, but he didn't. Instead, he just shrugged and pulled out his phone.

The rest of the morning went by like a blur. Quinn was flying out on their family jet that afternoon, so Winny and I fixed her some breakfast and spent the rest of the time chatting with her.

I couldn't help but feel like she lived a glamorous life. Nighttime parties. Celebrities. New York sounded amazing. When I commented on it, Quinn exclaimed that I needed to come visit.

Before I could even answer, Lucas snorted—loudly. I glared at him but if he noticed, he didn't respond.

Quinn ignored him and made me promise to come visit. Not

wanting to disappoint my new friend, I told her I'd think about it and that seemed to appease her.

Now she was gone and I was stuck with her crabby and rude twin. Score one for Lucas.

I groaned, drawing the attention of Maddie and Amber who were sitting at the table with me. They had been chatting about school starting in a week. It was our Senior year and it seemed like everyone else had their lives figured out but me.

Maddie was going to NCU and Amber was going to Duke. Me? I couldn't seem to bring myself to apply to any college. There was no way I was going to leave Dad and Drew. They needed me. Especially since Mrs. Protresca had left a very firm note on our door about the status of our yard.

It was only a matter of time before Dad ticked the city off and we were kicked out of our home.

"What's the matter with you?" Maddie asked, flicking her hair over her shoulder to study me.

I swallowed down the stress ball that rose up in my chest and shrugged as I fiddled with my straw. Truth was, I doubted my friends would understand what I was going through. They didn't have the problems I did.

They had mothers and fathers who didn't bring every piece of junk home with them. And they didn't have a ridiculously annoying, rich kid living at their job, interfering with every part of their lives or...walking across the rotunda right now.

I ducked behind my purse, trying to hide from Lucas.

He was talking to Wes and didn't seem to notice me. I held my breath as I watched them, praying that they would disappear before anyone else noticed them.

"Hey, isn't that the new rich kid?" Maddie asked and dread filled my chest.

Great. So much for staying hidden.

I shot Maddie an annoyed look and shook my head. "Yeah, but we don't have to say anything."

Maddie snorted. "Um, how is it that he looks even better *with* a shirt on?" She wiggled her eyebrows at Amber who just furrowed her brow.

"I've got to grab a new pair of shoes before practice gets brutal. I'll catch you guys later?" Amber asked, standing from the table and shooting me a sympathetic look.

"You don't have to go," I said, hoping she could hear the desperation in my voice.

"Lucas!" Maddie shouted and raised her hand.

Amber glanced between me, and Maddie and nodded. "Yeah. I promised my mom I'd be home in an hour." Then she leaned in. "Good luck."

I shot her a hurt look, but she just smiled and turned, making her way toward The Running Store.

Now alone with Maddie, I pulled my gaze up to see that Lucas and Wes had stopped and were staring at us.

"Come join us," Maddie said, waving toward the table.

Heat radiated from my body as I felt Lucas' eyes on me. Wes muttered something, but Lucas shook his head and started making his way toward us.

Why was he coming over here when he so obviously didn't like me? Why was he torturing me? It was so unfair.

"Hey, boys," Maddie said as they pulled out their chairs and sat.

"Hey Maddie. Charlotte," Wes said, nodding toward the both of us.

"Hey, Wes," I responded, purposely ignoring Lucas. When I did look over at him, I saw that he was smiling in his incredibly annoying way.

"What are you guys doing here?" Maddie asked, tucking her hair behind her ear and literally, batting her eyelashes as she stared at Lucas.

"We're, um…" Wes glanced over at Lucas as if he were waiting for permission to speak.

"Wes is showing me around. Trying to convince me that it's more than just a hill-billy town." Lucas leaned back with a satisfied look on his face.

Wes glanced at him with a strange look of his own. Like he didn't agree with what Lucas had just said.

But I knew Lucas, so what he said didn't surprise me. "Well, if you're not happy with living here, you can always leave. Sweet Water will find a way to survive without you." I glared at him. There was no way I was going to hide my distain for him anymore.

He was a jerk and I was going to let him know that.

"Char," Maddie said, shooting me an annoyed look. Then she turned back to Lucas and smiled. "Well, the mall doesn't do Sweet Water justice. You'll have to come to The Pier on Friday night. That's when Sweet Water gets wild." She leaned in and wiggled her eyebrows.

The Pier was what it sounded like. A pier that extended way out into the ocean. The water at the end was really deep and people would jump off it and into the ocean below. It was stupid and dangerous and something that I avoided, like the plague.

Wes nodded. "Yeah. It's pretty killer."

Lucas smiled as he glanced over at me for a moment before turning his attention back to Maddie. "If I'm here. I'm game."

"Great," Maddie smiled as she glanced down at her watch. "If we're going to make the movie, we should get going, Char."

I couldn't help the yawn that emerged. "I can't. I'm too tired. Plus, it's my night to babysit." I braced myself for Maddie's backlash.

She furrowed her brow at me and I could see the disappointment in her gaze.

"I'll go with you."

Lucas' response drew our attention over to him.

I stared at him. What was he doing? Was he serious?

"Really?" Maddie and Wes said in unison.

Lucas glanced between them and nodded. "Sure. I love the movies."

Maddie smiled and pushed her chair out. "Great. Um, let's go then."

Lucas stood and right before he turned to follow her, he glanced down at me and shot me a smile and a wink. "See you later, *Char*."

I glared at him, but he didn't respond. Instead, he called for Maddie to wait up and they both disappeared through the theater's doors on the other end of the rotunda.

I sat there, dumbfounded. I wasn't sure how I felt about my best friend and my new enemy hanging out together. In a movie. Where it was dark.

Ugh.

I swallowed as I forced a smile at Wes. He was staring at someone else. When I turned to see who, I saw Lauren Carmichael. She was a senior as well, and his neighbor. And from the look on his face, maybe more? Which was weird. Last I knew, he was dating Olivia. The self-proclaimed perfect girl of Sweet Water High.

"Everything okay, Wes?" I asked.

He snapped his attention back to me, and I swear his cheeks flushed.

"Yeah. Great." He shot me a sympathetic look. "I should go. I've got stuff to do."

I nodded. Typical. Everyone seemed to have something to do. Me? I was just trying to avoid my life right now.

"It's okay. You can go."

He stood, waved, and headed off in the direction that Lauren went.

I was going to have to ask her what that was about when I saw her next.

Not wanting to be a loser, sitting at the table alone, I shouldered my purse and headed toward the exit. Right now, getting as far way from the mall and Maddie and Lucas seemed like the best idea.

By the time I got home, I was exhausted. I said a quick hello to Dad and then climbed the stairs to my bedroom and slammed the door.

Two minutes later, I'd collapsed on my bed and sleep overtook me.

———

"Wake up!" Drew yelled.

I flipped to my side just in time to see Drew dive-bomb my bed. I raised my hands to protect myself, but his weight collapsed on me, and my breath left my body in a whoosh.

"Drew," I managed out. "You've got to stop doing that."

He just giggled and rolled around until he was off me but still laying on my bed, staring up at the ceiling.

"Dad told me to get you up. You napped too long. He's got to go to work."

I rubbed my eyes and yawned, nodding to no one in particular. It wasn't like Drew could see me. Maybe it was just to motivate myself to get up. "I'm up," I said, throwing the covers off and standing.

Drew buried himself in my comforter as I stretched and walked over to my bathroom to brush my teeth. They felt like something had died on them. Once I was minty fresh, I turned off my light to see that Drew had left.

Good. The last thing I needed was him messing up my room.

I made my way downstairs to see Dad standing next to the door, shoving his wallet into his back pocket. He glanced over at me and smiled. "You're in charge now, squirt. I'm out of here."

I saluted him and he grabbed the door handle. Just before he left, he paused. "I ordered pizza from Luigi's. It should have been here fifteen minutes ago, so you're going to have to handle the payment."

My stomach growled at the mention of food. "Gotcha," I said, as I made my way into the dining room to find Drew sitting at the table coloring a picture. My jaw dropped. That didn't happen very often. My brother usually tore through the house like a tornado.

And then I got closer and discovered what had his attention. He was coloring a picture of a dead squirrel with lots of blood gushing out of it.

Typical.

"Gross, Drew," I said as I made my way over to the kitchen and grabbed a glass and filled it with water.

Drew shrugged. "Dad says I have great attention to detail," he said as he scribbled the red crayon around on the paper. Right where the squirrel's head should be.

"I think you need to see a therapist," I muttered. Maybe we all needed to see a therapist. Especially since it seemed like we weren't dealing with Mom's death very well. Or even acknowledging it. Dad had even taken down all the pictures of her when she died.

It was like he was trying to erase her from our memory. It hurt. Both ways. Ignoring the pain and facing it.

I gulped the water, hoping it would push down the lump in my throat. But all it did was make me almost gag and leave me coughing. Drew raised his eyebrows at me and I just waved him off.

Once my coughing fit subsided, I wiped the tears that had formed on my eyes and cleared my throat. Just as I set my glass in the sink, the doorbell rang.

"I've got it," I rasped. I needed a distraction from my thoughts, plus, I had a feeling this was our pizza. Finally.

"Did you get lost?" I asked as I opened the door, and then

froze. I blinked a few times just to make sure that what I was looking at was actually real.

Lucas was standing on my doorstep with a Luigi's Pizza cap, shirt, and warming container in his hands. When his gaze landed on my face, his expression sank.

"Charlotte?"

"Lucas?"

We stared at each other for what felt like forever, before he pulled at the Velcro and removed our pizza boxes.

Not sure what was happening, I studied them. This felt like a trap. A pretty elaborate and strange trap, but a trap nonetheless.

"You ordered a pizza?" he asked.

I cleared my throat, forcing my thoughts to catch up with my mouth. "Yeah," I said slowly.

He glanced at the receipt. "Huh. It says Dirk Robinson."

"That's my dad."

He glanced up at me and then handed me the receipt. "Fine. It'll be $15.27."

I grabbed the twenty from the end table in our entryway and handed it over. "You can keep the change."

He took it and then placed the warmer under his arm as he shoved it into his back pocket. "I didn't know you lived in a scrap yard," he said, glancing behind him.

Heat rushed across my body. Of course he had to bring that up. "Yeah. My dad's a collector."

Lucas raised his eyebrows as he turned back to me. "Does he work on them?"

I nodded slowly, not sure where he was going with this.

"Huh," he said, and then made his way down the steps. "Enjoy your pizza," he called over his shoulder as he made his way to Winny's Suburban.

I stared at his retreating frame, so many questions rolling around in my mind.

I wanted to know how his movie went with Maddie. I wanted

to know when he started working at Luigi's. I wanted to know why a rich kid from New York even had needed a job in the first place. I wanted to know why he cared about the scrapyard outside of my house.

But most of all, I wanted to know why I cared at all.

CHAPTER SEVEN

*A*ll the questions that were floating around in my mind the night before were still plaguing me the next day when I pulled up behind The Bread Basket and parked my bike. Winny had called me before bed last night to ask if I'd come in and run the cash register in the afternoon.

It wasn't my favorite thing, but I agreed. She'd done so much for me that I felt bad turning her down.

So I slept in, which felt good. When I got downstairs, Dad was unusually giddy. I asked him what had happened and he told me that he had a potential buyer for his 1958 Chevy Impala. I just nodded, grateful at what this meant. Perhaps, if he could let go of one of the cars, he'd let go of all the cars.

And we'd get to stay in our house. We were a time bomb that was rapidly running out of seconds.

When I walked into the back of the bakery I found Winny standing there with her purse slung over her shoulder. She had on lipstick and looked more done up than I'd seen her look in...forever.

"Where are you off to looking so fancy?" I asked, hanging up my purse and slipping on my apron.

She gave me a nervous smile as she patted her hair that was styled up in a tight bun. "Is it too much?"

I shook my head. "You look beautiful."

A more confident smile emerged on her lips. "Oh, good." Then she leaned in. "I meeting my son at Alfonso's."

I let out a whistle. Alfonso's was the expensive Italian restaurant three towns over. "Pricey."

She nodded. But then a concerned look flashed in her eyes. Seeing that she needed a hug, I reached out and gave her a squeeze. "You'll be great. He's a fool not to mend whatever went wrong."

She hugged me back and then pulled away. "Thanks, Charlotte." Then she took a deep breath. "I should go before I'm late." She stepped past me and slipped outside.

I called another "Good luck" to her retreating frame and then shut the door behind her. After she pulled away, I made my way to the front. I stepped behind the register and fiddled with a few stacks of receipts, counted the cash, and restocked the rolls.

As is typical for a bakery at 2 o'clock in the afternoon, no one was around.

I settled onto the barstool behind the counter and grabbed out a book I kept stashed there. It was a total guilty pleasure but I loved the 1980's series, Sweet Valley High. They were so ridiculous, they were good. Like a soap opera for teenagers.

Just as I was engrossed in the story, the bell rattled on the door. I glanced up to see Lucas and...Maddie walking into the shop. I stared, dumbfounded at them as they seemed engrossed in whatever they were talking about.

The first thing I wanted to do was hide behind the counter. The second thing I wanted to do was get angry. Which was weird. Why was I so upset at the fact that they were together? They made a perfect couple.

I mean, they were both fancy. They both had money. And they

were both very self-involved—as hard as that was to say about my best friend.

They made sense. I should be happy for them. But I wasn't.

Lucas must have noticed me because his expression morphed into one I didn't recognize. He stepped away from Maddie and to the rye bread that was stacked in a basket against the far wall.

Maddie looked confused but when she turned and saw me, a smile formed on her lips. "Hey, Char," she said, stepping up to the counter.

I tried not to glare at her even though every muscle in my face wanted to. Why was I so angry that she was with Lucas? I should be fine with it. I wasn't interested in him like that.

So I forced my voice to come out normal and said, "Hey, Maddie. What are you doing here?"

She shrugged and played with the stack of iced sugar cookies on the counter. "Lucas and I ran into each other outside on the sidewalk."

Relief flooded my body. So they hadn't been hanging out. I could handle that. I felt a little less betrayed.

"Oh." I wasn't sure what to say. Any response sounded either lame or like I cared, so I decided to just nod.

Maddie glanced from me over to Lucas and then sighed. "Well, I should go." She gave me a smile. "I'll see you at The Pier tonight?"

My stomach twisted at the thought of jumping off the pier, but I didn't want to get into another round of 'why I am so lame' with Maddie, so I nodded. "Sure."

Her smiled broadened. "Perfect." Then she turned to Lucas who was watching us. "You coming?"

He glanced over at me, and then to Maddie. "I'll think about it."

She tucked her hair behind her ear and smiled. "I'd really love it if you came."

He just nodded and turned back around to focus on the bagged bagels.

Maddie looked hurt for a moment before she forced a smile. "I'll see you," she said.

I waved as she opened the door and disappeared around the corner.

Lucas and I were alone now and I wasn't sure what to do. Do I talk to him? Ignore him?

"How was your pizza?" he asked, turning around and facing me head on.

Well, at least I didn't have to figure out what I was supposed to say. Not with him taking charge of the conversation. I shrugged and ran my fingers over the register's keys. "Fine. Normal. What I expected."

Geez, why couldn't I just give him one answer?

He paused, I could have cut the tension with a knife.

"Aren't you going to ask me?"

I glanced over at him. "Ask you what?"

His expression turned strained. Like there was something bugging him. "Why a trust fund kid has to work at a pizza shop?"

I stared at him. "Why would I ask you that? Everyone needs a job. Luigi's is good. He's a fair boss and I'm sure you'll make good tips." Plus, I knew he was cut off from his family's fortune. So a job made sense and made him seem...human.

He studied me like I had two heads. Not sure how I felt about it, I dropped my gaze to my book, which I'd placed on the counter. Not wanting him to know my secret, I slipped it back into its hiding place.

When I glanced back up, he was a few feet beside me. I yelped as my heart jumped up into my throat. When did he get so close?

He raised his eyebrows as he studied me. Not sure what to say, I just stood there, staring back at him. He furrowed his brow. What was he thinking?

Then, feeling completely self-conscious, I reached up and casually rubbed my nose just in case I had something hanging from it.

"I can't figure you out," he muttered. But from the way he said it, it didn't sound like a question, just a fact.

I scoffed and stepped back, not sure how much I liked him being so close to me. "Me? There's not much to figure out."

He leaned against the counter and folded his arms. "What's your angle?"

"Angle? What?"

"Everyone has an angle. You're friend Maddie?" He motioned toward the front door. "She has a popularity angle."

I glanced in the direction of his gesture. My first reaction was to defend her, but the more I thought about it, the truer the words became. Maddie did want to be popular. In fact, it seemed to be her only concern nowadays. "Okay, true," I said.

Lucas waved his hand in my direction. "But you? What's your angle?" He leaned closer as if my answer was secretly written across my forehead in tiny lettering.

Feeling like I was suddenly in a guidance counselor meeting where I was supposed to declare what I wanted to do with the rest of my life, I swallowed hard. There was very little I understood about my life post-mom, and the last thing I wanted was someone dictating to me that I needed to know.

I glared at him. "Maybe some people don't have angles." Or don't know them. Anyway, why was he pushing this?

He shook his head. "Trust me, everyone has an angle."

Suddenly needing some fresh air, I stepped past him. "Well, maybe where you came from. But here, people are just trying to survive." I wrapped my arms around my chest and made my way back to the kitchen. "Watch the front for me," I called over my shoulder.

Once I was behind one of the big ovens, I let out the breath I'd been holding. It was my futile attempt to keep my emotions in check.

I leaned against the cool metal as I took in a few deep breaths. I needed to stop freaking out. I'm sure Lucas didn't mean what I interpreted his questions to mean. I just needed to get a grip. I was just so unnerved when I was around him.

I wiped at my cheeks to make sure I had no escaping tears and then moved to leave my hiding place. When I rounded the corner, I saw Lucas standing there, looking as if he wasn't sure what to say.

When he saw me, he dropped his gaze. "I, um, I didn't mean to upset you," he said.

I stared at him, not sure what he was getting at. But, instead of focusing on it, I took a deep breath and forced a smile. "I'm fine. See, totally fine." I waved toward my body.

He raised his eyes to study me. Then he reached out and ran his fingers on the countertop. "This is all new to me," he said, his voice so low that I wasn't 100% sure he'd said anything.

I wanted to ask him what he meant, but I decided against it. Instead, I just watched him, waiting for him to continue.

"In the world I come from, everyone has an agenda. They always want something from me...no matter the cost." He glanced up at me and for the first time, I saw something I didn't think Lucas was capable of feeling.

Pain.

I nodded. That was a feeling I could understand. It was human. It was raw and it made Lucas vulnerable. "Not here. Most people are just trying to survive whatever messed up life they are living," I answered, hoping he'd understand that maybe *most people,* really just meant me.

He nodded and blew out his breath in slow motion. "I know. I'm beginning to understand that." Then he scoffed and a smile emerged on his lips. "It's strange."

We stood in silence for what felt like an eternity until the bell that hung from the front door jingled. I gave him a quick smile, and headed to help the customer that walked in.

I was grateful for the distraction my job gave me. I needed a break from Lucas and the confusing feelings that were starting to burn in my stomach.

Life was easier when Lucas was this spoiled kid who didn't know how to be a decent human being. But now that he was being somewhat nice, it was...disconcerting.

After I helped Mrs. Bryant, the preacher's wife, with her order for rolls after Sunday service, I waved to Jett—her son, whom I assumed she'd dragged along, judging by the look on his face—as they walked out the door.

Now alone, I took a deep breath and turned to see that Lucas had come back into the shop, but instead of standing dangerously close to me like he did on a regular basis, he was sitting on one of the shop's chairs. He was focused on his phone with a strained expression as he scrolled his screen with his finger.

Taking a chance on our newfound...friendship, I rested my elbows on the counter and glanced over at him. "Everything okay?" I asked. Being bold felt good and terrifying at the same time.

He snapped his attention over to me and swallowed, his jaw clenching from the movement. "Yeah. I'm fine."

"You don't look it," I said, hoping my playful tone came across as I intended.

He stood and shoved his phone into his back pocket. "Well, I am." He made his way to the back, pausing before pushing through the swinging door. "Besides, how do you know? We've just met. Like you said, you don't know me." His words lingered in the air as he glanced down at me.

I furrowed my brow as I studied his now hardened gaze.

Wow. Talk about Dr. Jekyll and Mr. Hyde. I glared at him. "Excuse me for caring, but I thought that's what friends do."

He shook his head. "That's your first mistake, assuming we were friends." He set his jaw as he pushed through the door and disappeared into the back.

For some reason, my heart felt as if it were breaking. Which is stupid. I should be glad that spoiled, rich kid didn't want to be my friend. After all, what did I have to offer him? Nothing.

Just like he had nothing to offer me.

The sooner I got that through my head, the better.

CHAPTER EIGHT

*T*he rest of my shift at The Bread Basket was awkward and strained. Lucas eventually came back down but instead of talking to me, he stayed in the back, drinking coffee while eating the defective cookies and brooding.

Whatever happened between him and I, or between him and his phone, left him in an extremely sour mood.

Instead of being at the receiving end of his backlash, I just stayed in the front, with people who actually wanted to see me and talk to me.

When Winny got back, she looked sad. I wanted to ask how the lunch date went, but she gave me a look that said she really didn't want to talk about it and I could respect that.

So I gave her a supportive hug and then rushed outside to my bike. It was the first time in a long time that I was actually grateful to be going home. The Bread Basket was slowly turning into a torture chamber instead of an escape.

If only Lucas and I could figure out our crap, things could get back to normal. Or if he'd just leave—I'd take that too.

After a few relaxing hours at home—thankfully, Drew got invited to spend the night at his friend's house—I eventually peeled myself off my couch and got ready. At seven o'clock sharp, I stood outside my house, waiting for Maddie to pick me up. I'd kept the promise to go with her even though every part of me wanted to head straight back into my house and hide out under my covers.

Maddie honked a few times before pulling up to our house and letting her engine idle. I swung open the passenger door and smiled down at her.

"You are actually coming," she said as I slipped onto the seat and buckled.

I shot her an annoyed look. "What does that mean?"

She scoffed. "It means that you're always making excuses."

"Am not."

She studied me. "Are to. All you want to do is hang out at your house or the bakery." Then she sighed. "Which now that Lucas is staying there, I get that, but you need to live your life." She studied me before merging onto the road. "It's what your mom would have wanted you to do."

My stomach twisted at the mention of my mom. This was not how I wanted to spend the evening. Especially when the one person who could give me advice about what my mom would want, was sitting next to me. She was there for me through the illness and death. I almost *had* to listen to what she said. After all, Maddie seemed to be the only person who wanted to talk about Mom.

Maddie may not be perfect, but she was the closest thing to a support system I had. And there was nothing that was going to get in the way of that. Especially not me and my stupidity.

"I know. I'm trying. I'm here, right?" I gave her a soft smile, hoping to appease her.

She furrowed her brow and then drove away from the curb. "You're right. You're here. I can be happy."

I nodded as I settled back into my chair. Grateful that I

avoided a fight, I smiled over at her. She started talking about Lucas and the fun they had at the movie.

I tried not to wince as she went into detail about how his arm brushed against hers and how she thought he was going to kiss her. Halfway through her story I almost asked her to go back to talking about my mom. For some reason, the thought of the two of them together made me want to vomit...or cry. Either way, it was uncomfortable and I hated it.

It must have been the fact that I knew more about Lucas than she did and yet, she had a different view of his personality than me. Why was he nice to her and mean to me? What did I ever do to him?

The car had grown quiet and I realized that Maddie had stopped talking. I turned to see her studying me.

"What?" I asked.

She snorted. "Geez, off in la-la land?"

I furrowed my brow. "What?"

"I asked you if Lucas ever talks about me."

I cleared my throat and shifted in my seat. I didn't like this whole 'being the middle' person between them. There were many reasons why, some of which I just couldn't quite figure out myself, so felt it best to keep quiet.

"Um, yeah. Sort of." I didn't really remember but I also didn't want to hurt her feelings. Truth was, Lucas and I really didn't have time to chat, much less talk about his feelings for her. Which I doubted he'd even share with me if I asked.

"Wow. That's specific," she said, glancing over at me as she idled at a stoplight.

I shrugged. "Lucas isn't a big talker."

She sighed and turned left when the light shifted to green. "Yeah, I got that too." She peeked over at me. "Will you ask him about me?"

My stomach twisted at her questions. Did I want to talk to him about her? No. Not at all. Hopefully, it was because I didn't really want to talk to Lucas at all and not the fact that I didn't like the idea of Lucas liking anyone, much less my best friend.

He was too confusing.

"Um, sure," I lied. Man, I was the worst. But if Lucas was interested in her, he didn't seem like the kind of guy who would wait around. If he'd just make his move already, I wouldn't have to deal with all of her questions and I'd know where we stood.

The grin on her face literally lit up the entire car. I tried to meet her enthusiasm as she started talking about how she couldn't wait for school to start so she could see him more.

Great. This was the absolute worst thing that could be happening. Lucas was infiltrating every part of my life and I wasn't sure how I felt about any of it.

All I knew was, right now, I hated it.

We filled the rest of the time with conversations about school and who we wanted for our teachers. I was grateful for the break from our conversation about Lucas—except for the fact that every few seconds, his annoying smile and face made its way into my thoughts.

It took some effort, but I managed to force it out, which meant that by the time Maddie pulled into the Pier's parking lot, I was exhausted.

I could see our group gathered at the very end of the pier, goofing off. Suddenly, I regretted coming here. It was foolish and dangerous and right now, losing me was the last thing my family needed.

I swallowed against the lump in my throat. How the heck was I going to get out of this?

Maddie patted my hand as she swung her door open and climbed out. "Come on. It'll be fun. Stop being morbid."

Well, that was one reason why we were friends. She could literally read my mind.

"I'm not being morbid."

She shot me a look that told me that she didn't believe me. I forced a smile just to support my reaction.

"Come on. You're only a teenager once."

Yeah, and I wanted to get to adulthood too. But I kept that thought to myself. I didn't need her telling me that I was acting like an old lady.

So, against my will, I climbed out of the car and took a deep breath. I could do this. Before mom, I was an adventurous person. Now? A cave away from the world sounded like the best place to spend my time. Maybe it was because once you suffer from a death like I did, you suddenly realize how precious life is.

And being stupid didn't sound that appealing.

There was a whoop from the group when we met up with them. Maddie half-sauntered and half-danced her way over to them and they literally swallowed her up.

I kept to the outskirts of the circle, still not sure if I really wanted to do this. I mean, I didn't want to do this, but I didn't want to be that loser friend.

"Nervous?"

I yelped and turned around to see Lucas standing behind me. He was leaning against the railing with his hands shoved into his pockets. He had on a black t-shirt and swim trunks. I couldn't tell if he was excited or nervous—or maybe he just didn't care.

Either way, he didn't look like he was a mess like I was. How could he be so relaxed? Especially since he seemed so panicked when he thought I was drowning.

Lucas was a mystery that I was beginning to think I was never going to figure out.

"N-no, you?" Wow. Way to have confidence.

His eyebrows rose as he glanced behind me toward the expansive ocean and then back to my face. "Nah. I've jumped off higher places before."

"Really?" Why was I surprised? I'm sure he went to the fjords and jumped off them. After all, he was rich. "I mean, that sounds about right."

He studied me. "What does that mean?"

I cleared my throat as I rubbed my arms. I wasn't cold but it seemed as if all my anxiety was manifesting itself in shivers. "Well, you're rich." I winced. Was that bad to say even if it was true?

He scoffed. "Not really. My parents are rich. I've been cut off." He shoved his hands through his hair as he blew out his breath.

I watched him, not sure what I was supposed to say to that. Agree? Disagree? I was just shocked that he was even talking to me about something personal and I really didn't want to stop him. So, I pinched my lips shut and let him continue.

"Well, cut off until I come back to the model Addington that my dad wants me to be."

Hmm, what could he have done that was so disappointing to his parents? "What did you do?" escaped before I could force the question back down.

He furrowed his brow but before he could answer, Maddie sauntered over to him and wrapped her arm around his waist. "There you are," she said, smiling up at him.

Lucas stiffened and flicked his gaze over at me. I pretended like I didn't notice. Did he not like Maddie or was he embarrassed that he was now dating my best friend? Either way, I decided that it was best to just ignore what was happening in front of me. I didn't care. Right?

"So, are you going to jump with me?" she asked, reaching up and running her hand over his chest.

Wow. My friend was really forward. Or maybe they did have that kind of relationship. Who was I to judge?

Spotting Amber, I waved at her and made my way over. I really didn't want to watch Lucas and Maddie have a moment.

I stepped up to her. "Hey."

She smiled. "Hey. Didn't expect to see you here."

I shrugged. "Maddie forced me."

She chuckled. "Yeah. Sounds like Maddie."

I sighed and glanced around. "So are we really going to do this?"

"Sure. Why not?"

Realizing that I might be the only one with death on her mind, I just shrugged. "No reason." I didn't want to be the killjoy at this party.

Couples began to line up, each stripping down to their swimsuits and designating Tammy as the person to bring them over to the roaring bonfire on the beach. I wanted to volunteer as tribute to be the runner, but she agreed first. I was stuck at the top, staring down to what seemed like the thing that was going to end my life.

I tried to remain calm as I glanced at the other kids around me. How were they so calm? They were patiently waiting as the first group dove off the side and from their stoic faces, they were not the nervous jumble of nerves like I was.

It only got worse as I watched the line grow shorter and shorter.

At first, I pretended to be focused on my phone. Then, I moved to stretching and slipping out of my clothes and down to my black one-piece.

Once there were only a few stragglers left, I decided it was time to get in line and get this over with.

There were only two couples in front of me and my heart started to pound. I was actually going to do this. For some reason, I wanted to write a goodbye note to Dad and Drew just incase I didn't make it. Plus, it didn't help that I was jumping alone. Everyone else seemed to have another person to pair up with— and I was trying to ignore the fact that Maddie and Lucas had paired up pretty fast. Apparently, I'd been too focused on delaying the inevitable that I missed that window and now, I was forced to go solo.

The couple on the edge jumped, leaving one couple between

me and the plummet. I felt as if my heart was about to gallop out of my chest. Panic raced throughout my body and it was taking all my strength not to run as far away from this place as my legs could carry me.

Where was Maddie? She forced me to come here only to ditch me for Lucas. The couple in front of me jumped, leaving me...alone.

I shivered as I peered over the ledge to see the waves crashing against the legs of the pier. What was I doing? Why was I here? Would anyone even notice if I didn't jump?

Probably not.

I gripped my glasses as I rationalized leaving. I was freaking myself out for nothing. There was no harm in just calling it quits and turning around. Wasn't my safety important? People would understand, and if they didn't, I could always play the dead mom card. That was sure to get me some pity.

Just as I was about to turn around and run away, a somewhat warm and wet hand engulfed mine. Startled, I glanced up to see Lucas standing next to me. He was sopping wet. His hair dripped with water and his skin glistened in the moonlight.

I couldn't help but stare at him. What was he doing?

"I figured you didn't want to go alone," he said, keeping his gaze trained on the water below.

"I—you—" I pinched my lips together as I forced a coherent thought, it came out in one word, "Thanks."

He shrugged and pulled me to the edge. "It's just a jump. Don't read into this."

I couldn't help the smile that played on my lips. Sure. Let him think that. He glanced over at me and counted down to one.

Just as he yelled, "Jump," we both leapt off the pier and plunged into the water still holding hands.

CHAPTER NINE

*T*he water surrounded me as I sunk down under the surface. For some reason, the fear that was crippling me earlier had disappeared. A sense of satisfaction filled my chest as I kicked hard to the surface.

This was the first spontaneous thing I'd done since Mom. And it felt great.

When I broke the surface, I searched the water for Lucas. He was a few feet away, looking as if he were doing the same. When he saw me, he swam toward me.

He bobbed up and down in the water as he stared at me. Geez, he looked good wet. Water droplets clung to his hair and eyelashes. The moon's light shone down, illuminating him. Did I look this amazing wet? Probably not.

"You survived," he said, wrapping a hand around my arm and pulling me closer to him.

My heart sped up from the feeling of his touch. His grip was firm and strong. As if letting me go was the last thing he wanted to do. And if I was honest with myself, I never wanted him to let me go. Which was strange for me to feel.

"I survived," I said, shaking my glasses off and slipping them on so I could see better and then I turned to study him. Feelings bubbled to the surface and I tried to swallow them down. What was going on? Why was he confusing me at every turn? "Why did you come back?"

His expression turned serious as he let go of me and flipped to his back. I swam alongside of him as the sound of another couple splashing into the water filled the air. Once we were a safe distance, he turned to face me. "You looked a bit panicked," he said.

Wow. Mr. Snobby, rich kid was worried about me?

"And you're about my only friend here. I couldn't have you dying on me, could I?" He shrugged like that was the most logical reason for his attempt to rescue me.

And there it was. The real reason. I was the only one who was putting up with his attitude and he didn't want to be alone when school started. There were always ulterior motives when it came to Lucas—or that was the answer I needed to cling to because any other reason made me feel vulnerable.

"Nice," I said, turning to my side to get ready to swim away.

"Hey. Wait," he said, reaching out and grabbing my hand. When he pulled me closer, water splashed up on my face.

He held me up in the water until my coughing fit subsided. I glared at him. "Will you stop doing that? You think you're saving me but really, you're just water boarding me."

He chuckled, but still kept his arm firmly wrapped around my waist. Heat radiated from every point of contact. I never realized how much warmth a guy's bare chest generated.

It actually made the summer heat feel cool.

When he didn't let me go, I peered up at him. What was he thinking? Why was he such a mystery?

He was watching me with a funny look in his eyes. Like he was trying to figure out the same thing.

"Charlotte?"

I swallowed, not sure if I wanted to know what he was about

to ask me. But, curiosity won out and I said, "Yeah?"

He closed his lips like he was trying to gather his thoughts. "I, um—"

"Lucas!"

We both turned to see Maddie wading out into the water. She was waving her arms like a crazy person.

Lucas looked back at me. "She can wait," he said.

Wow. He was making me a priority over Maddie? "It's okay, you can go," I said, pushing against his very firm chest to break the hold he had on me.

"Your phone is ringing!" Maddie called. "It says dad."

Lucas cursed under his breath.

Taking this moment to halt whatever was happening between us, I let out a small laugh and swam a few feet from him. "It's really no big deal. I'm fine. Remember? Swim team."

He watched my retreat, but I could tell that he wanted to finish what he was about to say to me. Truth was, I didn't want to hear it anymore. Not now, not ever.

I was fine with our relationship and the way it was. There was no need to confuse each other.

By the time I got to the beach, I pulled myself from the water and walked up the sand. Maddie was standing there, watching me with a confused look on her face.

I gave her a quick smile and headed over to where I left my clothes. Once I was dressed, I made my way to the table that had been set up. A bonfire had been started and kids were hanging out, either wrapped up with their significant other, or talking. Not sure what I should do, I grabbed a Ginger Ale and made my way over to a stump and sat down.

After checking my phone to see I didn't have any missed texts or phone calls, I shoved my phone back into my pocket, cursing my boring life. What I wouldn't give to get the heck out of here and curl up in my bed where everything made sense.

Or at least, wasn't so confusing.

Maddie sat down next to me, a disgruntled look on her face. I gave her a fake smile, hoping she didn't want to talk about why Lucas and I had been in the ocean. If I were honest with myself, I really didn't even know.

"So, what's going on with you and Lucas?" she asked, turning to give me her full attention.

My hope that we could move on from talking about him floated away with the wind.

"Nothing. He just—I just—" I sighed. Not sure what I really wanted to say.

Her eyebrows had furrowed as she stared at me. "That didn't look like nothing."

I pushed my feet out, watching the sand gather around them. "I'm not sure what it looked like, but I can promise you that there's nothing going on from my end. I hate him." The last sentence didn't feel like the truth I'd held onto since I met him. Sure I disliked him, but hate might be a strong word.

Maddie looked a little more convinced as she processed my words. Then she laughed and flicked her hair over her shoulder. "Of course. I'm so sorry. I just really like him, you know?" Her gaze made it's way over to Lucas who was standing about fifty feet off, studying his phone.

I glanced over at him as well, and butterflies began to assault my stomach. Great. This was not good. Not good at all. "Well, he's an idiot if he doesn't feel the same."

She smiled back at me. "Really? You think so?"

I forced out the pain that was squeezing my chest. Instead, I nodded and wrapped my arm around her shoulders, giving her a squeeze. "Definitely. You're a catch. Most of the guys in Sweet Water would battle to the death for you."

She laughed, throwing her head back. "This is why we are best friends."

From the corner of my eye, I saw Lucas glance over at us. Despite the fact that I wanted to turn around to see who he was staring at—me or Maddie—I didn't. Truth was, I didn't want to know either way.

If it was Maddie, I was pretty sure my pounding heart couldn't handle it.

If it was me, I was pretty sure it would change my relationship with my best friend forever.

Neither of those situations sounded good to me. So I decided to stay in the dark.

After a quick hug, Maddie stood and made her way over to the clump of cheerleaders standing by the bonfire. Now alone, I wrapped my arms around my chest and stared at the flames. My emotions were everywhere, making my stomach hurt.

Since when did my life become so messy? I'd tried so hard not to involve myself in situations where I could come out hurt. I was still healing from Mom. This was the last thing I needed.

"Can I sit?"

Lucas' deep, smooth voice surrounded me, giving me goosebumps. I closed my eyes for a moment, reveling in the idea of saying yes. Of letting him sit next to me. To maybe care about me?

But I couldn't do that. I couldn't say yes and have another person who means so much to me get angry about the choice I made. So I set my jaw and turned my gaze up to him.

"What are you doing?"

He furrowed his brow. "What?"

I stood, and despite the fact that my heart was pounding, I held my ground. "You flirt with my friend, and then with me? What's your angle?" I jutted out my finger and poked his chest.

He reached up and grabbed my hand. In one swift movement, he pulled me close to him. "What are you talking about?"

My head swam from his proximity. Everything that I was trying to force myself not to feel for him was overpowering my senses. I needed to get away from him, but my legs wouldn't listen.

"You said everyone has an angle. I'm just trying to figure out what yours is."

He stared down at me. I felt raw and exposed from his gaze. How could one looked pierce my soul? I hated it. I wanted to stay hidden. I didn't want anyone to see me—much less the trust-fund kid who blew in here and was most likely going to leave just as fast.

"Why would you think I have an angle with you?" He studied me and the depth of his voice caused my toes to tingle.

I wiggled until he let me go. I needed to get away from him. "Because everyone does, and you're no different." I turned and walked through the sand, my feet sinking with each step.

I heard him call out my name, but I ignored him. Staying here was the last thing I wanted to do. I grabbed my phone out of my pocket and texted Maddie that I found a ride home. I used Drew as an excuse for the reason I needed to leave. After I slipped on my shoes, I headed down the road, keeping to the shoulder to avoid getting hit.

Luckily, only crazy teenagers would be at the beach this late, so the road was dead. I wrapped my arms around my chest as I fought the urge to dissect what had just happened. What was Lucas's deal? Why couldn't he just leave me alone?

He and Maddie were so perfect together. I couldn't understand why he wanted to be near me when he could have her.

I groaned as I tipped my face up to the dark sky. The stars shone down on me. "Why me?" I called out, reaching my arms out.

Tears filled my eyes as I thought of Mom. Was she watching me? Did she know what was happening? Did she care? If she were still around, I would curl up with her and tell her all my problems. She would call me her sugar-pop as she ran her fingers through my hair.

Then she would tell me some detailed story about a girl she once knew. I'd only half-listen, but by the end, I would come away feeling like Mom told me exactly what I needed to hear. She'd help me sort through my problem by not fixing my problem.

I needed her more than ever.

I wiped at my tears, feeling ridiculous for crying, and focused on the road in front of me. Ten minutes later, I was regretting my hiatus from the party. My feet hurt. I was wet and cold. And I had another forty-five-minute walk just to get to the outskirts of town.

Two head lights drew my attention backward and I squinted against their glare. It wasn't until the vehicle was slowing to a stop that I realized it was Winny's car. Which could only mean one thing. Lucas.

I shivered and turned, wrapping my arms tighter around my chest. That was the last thing I wanted to do. Climb into a car with him.

I heard the driver's door slam and the sound of crunching gravel grew louder. A hand grabbed my arm, halting my retreat.

"What the heck are you doing?" Lucas' voice was low and full of irritation.

I swallowed and turned, forcing a relaxed, go-with-it vibe. "I was walking," I said.

His jaw was set and his brows furrowed. "Are you serious? Do you want to get kidnapped?"

I scoffed and shifted, hoping he'd let go of my arm. I hated how I reacted to his touch. I wasn't supposed to. He was Maddie's —not mine. I shouldn't be feeling anything but frustration for him. But from the worried expression he was giving me, the butterflies in my stomach were going crazy.

He dropped his hand and pushed it through his hair. He turned and I watched as his shoulder rose and fell. Wow. He was really worried about me.

It was cute and weird at the same time. For a guy who acted like he hated me half the time, seeing him all bent out of shape because I decided to walk home from the party was strange.

He turned and his frustration seemed to have dissipated. Instead, he just looked exhausted. "Can I give you a ride home?"

I peered back in the direction of the party. "What about Maddie?" I asked. I wanted to sound confident and like I didn't care, but my voice betrayed me.

He shrugged. "She's having a lot of fun without me." He looked at me, and the intensity of his gaze made my heart pick up speed. "Besides, Winny would kill me if I let anything happen to her best employee."

I raised my eyebrows. "Did she say that specifically? I mean, did she say the words *best employee?*"

He chuckled. "Maybe not exactly, but I can tell from the way she acts around you." His expression softened. "You're something special."

Heat raced across my skin and settled on my cheeks as I studied him. Was *he* saying that? Or Winny? Too nervous to even ask, I sighed and nodded, "Fine. I'll let you take me home." I walked over to the car.

Just as I neared the door, Lucas beat me to it, reaching out and pulling on the handle before I even had a chance. I glanced up at him, my breath catching in my throat. He was inches from me. Was it wrong that I loved how much he towered over me? That I felt tiny in his presence?

And then I scolded myself. Yes. That was wrong.

I reached out to grab the seat, but Lucas' hand met mine instead. Warmth radiated up my arm as the thought to drop his hand raced through my mind. Then realizing how exposed that might make me, I gripped it as I climbed inside.

"Thanks," I mumbled, not wanting to meet his gaze.

He nodded and shut the door once I was situated. Then he jogged around the hood of the car and climbed into the driver's seat.

After he started the car, he took off down the road. I sat there, not sure what to say or what to do. I swallowed down the unsettling feelings that were rising up in my chest. What was happening?

CHAPTER TEN

We drove in silence through the streets of downtown Sweet Water. I kept glancing over at Lucas, wondering what he was thinking. Then I'd curse myself for even caring.

He pulled up into my driveway and let the engine idle as he turned to look at me.

"Everything okay?" he asked. His forehead was furrowed as he studied me.

I chewed my lip and nodded. Of course, things weren't okay. But I wasn't going to tell him that. I wasn't sure I was ready to be vulnerable at all—much less express my confusing feelings to him. "Yeah, of course. Why wouldn't they be?"

His furrow deepened as he kept his gaze trained on my face. "You're just acting…strange."

Great. This was not what I wanted. I forced a smile and turned to face him. "Strange? Hmm…maybe you're just learning my personality."

He grew quiet and I felt as if I were melting under his stare. Why did things have to be so confusing?

"Charlotte—" he started at the same time I said, "Lucas—"

We both pinched our lips together as our eyes met. I gave him a look that I hoped said, 'leave it alone'. He studied me before sighing and straightening in his seat with both of his hands on the steering wheel.

"I'll see you tomorrow," he said. He kept his concentration on the dashboard in front of him.

I wanted to explain what was going on with me. I didn't want him to think that I hated him. It was just, with him, things were confusing. And right now, I couldn't handle confusing. Especially when my best friend was mixed up in all of this.

So I sighed and grabbed the door handle. "Thanks for giving me a ride a home. You saved me a lot of blisters."

He nodded and I felt his gaze fall on me as I climbed out. Once I was on the ground, I slammed the door closed, gave him a final wave, and turned to make my way up to my front door. Just before I slipped into my house, I glanced behind me to see him watching me.

His brows were furrowed and I could tell something was bothering him. And, for some reason, I let myself care. Really care. I wanted to fix whatever frustration he was feeling. I wanted to understand what was happening to me. But I couldn't.

Not right now.

So I gave him a friendly wave and made my way inside and shut the door. Now in the safety of my house, I turned and rested my back against the door. After a few deep breaths...I didn't feel better. If anything, I felt worse.

After kicking off my flip-flops and heading upstairs, I jumped into the shower to wash the salt water and sand off. Once I was clean, I dressed in pajamas and curled up on my bed.

I grabbed a book off my nightstand and flipped it open. Just as I finally disappeared into the words, my phone chimed. I picked it up to see that it was a text from Winny.

SOS Dough for the rolls didn't rise. Need help.

I glanced at the time. 10 o'clock.

MISUNDERSTANDING THE BILLIONAIRE'S HEIR | 75

Sighing, I pulled off my covers, dressed in a dark purple t-shirt and overalls, grabbed my glasses and headed downstairs. I left a quick note for Dad, telling him where I was, and then headed out back to grab my bike.

Ten minutes later, I pulled into the back of The Bread Basket and parked my bike.

After I climbed off, I headed into the shop, stopping just inside to grab my apron. I stilled my nerves as I rounded the corner of the kitchen. It was ridiculous to think that Lucas would be down here. After all, he wasn't the least bit interested in baking. He'd made that pretty clear since he got here.

No, tonight was just going to be about me and Winny. If I were honest with myself, I was really excited for a baking break.

Winny was standing in the middle of the kitchen, staring into one of her big, metal bread bowls. She looked like she was on the brink of tears.

"What happened?" I asked, walking up to her and peering over her shoulder.

She tipped the bowl toward me so I could see the pathetic mound of dough at the bottom. "I guess I forgot the yeast," she said in a half-laugh, half-whisper.

I patted her shoulder. "Don't worry, we'll get this fixed."

She shot me a huge smile. "I knew I could depend on you, Charlotte. You've always been there for me." Then she sighed. "It wouldn't be such a big deal if they weren't needed right away tomorrow morning. I love the church but man, they'll have us working all night."

I nodded as I headed over to the mixing bowl and started measuring out the flour. Just as I dumped the second scoop in, a clattering sound caused me to jump. I whipped around to see Winny staring down at the bowl she'd just dropped. I studied her. Never before had I seen her so stressed out.

What was going on? It seemed that ever since Lucas came to town, Winny had changed. She looked so tired and defeated and I wondered if the appearance of Lucas' dad had anything to do with it.

Realizing she was no good to me down here, I walked over, grabbed the bowl from the floor, and dumped it into the sink. "Go upstairs," I said, waving my hand in the direction of her apartment.

She raised her eyebrows. "Excuse me?"

I placed both hands on my hips and focused my gaze. "You forgot the yeast in the bread, Winny. I don't think you've ever done that. I don't need you messing up again." I gave her a soft smile. "Go upstairs, take a bath, and get some sleep. I'll take care of the rolls."

She rubbed her temples and sighed. "But—"

I shook my head, stepped up to her and pressed my hands on her shoulders, nudging her in the direction of the stairs. "It won't take me too long. I could make these in my sleep. I've got it covered. Go upstairs and take a break."

Her shoulders slumped as she gave in to my insistence. As she climbed the stairs, she glanced behind her in my direction. "Thanks, Charlotte."

I nodded and watched until she was out of view. Finally alone, I made my way to the mixing bowl and resumed measuring.

Only two minutes had passed before I heard footsteps on the stairs. Turning and preparing myself for a fight with Winny, I stopped when I saw Lucas. He was in a pair of flannel pajama bottoms and a white t-shirt. My heart leapt in my chest at the sight of him.

Hoping my reaction wasn't written all over my face, I turned and focused on the salt I was now dumping into the mixture. "I'm really fine. You can go back upstairs," I said, not wanting to turn to see where he was.

"Winny demanded that I come down here," he said, his voice inches from my ear.

I shivered. My body yearned for but also hated how close he

was to me. Why did I keep reacting this way? Man, I was a glutton for punishment.

"I'm really okay," I said, this time, not as confident.

"I know," he said, low and smooth.

I wanted to turn around. I wanted to ask him what everything between us meant. But I was too scared. I liked not knowing. It was safe. I was safe. There was no way I could get hurt when I was in the dark about everything.

He stood behind me for a few seconds before asking, "Anything I can do to help?"

I looked down at the sugar I was about to measure out. "Do you know anything about baking rolls?"

"No. But you could teach me."

I turned to see his earnest smile. It was almost like...he was trying. Why?

I cleared my throat and grabbed the recipe card from the counter. "It's not rocket science. You just measure out the ingredients and stir."

He took the paper from me, brushing his fingers against mine in the processes. Crackles of electricity raced up my arm from the contact. My breath hitched in my throat as I dropped my gaze to our hands.

It felt as if he lingered against my skin for a bit longer than necessary. Was that purposeful? I blinked a few times, hoping to remove that ridiculous thought and dropped my hand.

"Charlotte..." he started and stopped as if he wanted me to react.

"I'm going to grab the eggs," I said, sidestepping him and heading toward the fridge.

He didn't respond, which I was grateful for. I didn't need him talking to me right now. Anything he had to say to me would either break my heart or change our relationship forever. I wasn't sure which one I wanted or if I wanted anything at all.

Gah. Why did I have to feel so confused all the time?

By the time I got back, Lucas had a very wide and confident grin on his lips. He turned and wiggled his eyebrows.

"You looked satisfied with yourself," I said, as I set the carton of eggs on the counter.

He shrugged. "I measured the sugar."

I peered down into the bowl and saw the mound of sugar inside of it. "Wow," I said, glancing up. "That's amazing."

He shot me a look that told me he wasn't amused by reaction. "Well, for someone who only knows how to boil water, this is a big step for me."

I opened the carton of eggs as his statement rolled around in my mind. "Do you only eat pasta?"

"What?"

"Well, it's either pasta or boiled eggs."

Our conversation paused and when I glanced up at Lucas, he was watching me with a confused look. Then, recognition passed over his face and he chuckled.

"My family has a chef."

Ah. Of course. He was rich. "Right."

I started to crack the eggs into a bowl. He reached out to still my hand. "What does that mean?" he asked. For some reason, his voice had gotten deeper. Worried.

I glanced up at him and shrugged. "Nothing. Just a reminder of how different our worlds are."

He furrowed his brow as he studied me. "Different?"

I nodded. "Yeah, you know. You live at the Ritz and I live in a house that doubles as a scrap yard." I pulled my hand free and cracked another egg, all the while, cursing myself. What was I doing? Why was I opening up to this guy?

He probably didn't care. No, not probably. He *didn't* care. Why would he?

"So, is your dad like, a car junkie?"

I peeked over to see him grab an egg and tap it on the edge of the bowl. He finally got the shell open only to fling a few pieces inside of the bowl.

I tsked and reached in to fish out the shell. "The goal isn't to make crunchy rolls."

He cleared his throat and muttered an apology. When I glanced over, I saw that his cheeks had flushed. Feeling as if I had completely embarrassed him, I grabbed another egg and held it out for him.

"Try again."

He looked up and took the egg from me. Our fingers most definitely brushed against each other and I didn't pull away. Instead, I held his gaze as I let my fingers linger next to his.

His half-smile tugged at his lips. "Like this?" he asked, moving the egg until its top hovered right on the edge of the bowl.

"It's better to use the longer side," I said, reaching out and moving the egg for him. He leaned in to me, and I felt his chest brush against my shoulder. His face was inches from mine. "Now tap it a few times." I wrapped my hand around his and tapped the egg on the edge of the bowl.

Was it wrong that I loved the feeling of his skin against mine? It was warm and it wasn't until now that I realized how big his hands were. Or how perfect it felt to stand there with his body so close to mine.

It had been so long since I'd felt this close to someone. And I loved it. No. I craved it. I didn't want it to ever end.

He wrapped his other arm around me and suddenly, my entire back was pressed against his chest. I didn't flinch or pull back. Instead, I guided his hand up to the egg and together, we pulled the shell apart.

"Nice," I said as the egg slid into the bowl.

He chuckled and I could feel it through his chest. "I had a good teacher."

I shrugged as I took the shells from him. "Well, eggs aren't the hard part of baking." I pushed against his arm and he moved so I could slip the shell into the garbage.

When I got back, Lucas was cracking another egg. I felt a little disappointed that he was so confident to do it on his own. I kind of wanted to replay what had happened over and over again until all the eggs in Winny's kitchen had been cracked.

But, if I asked, he'd know that I wanted to be close to him. There was no way he could find out that when I was around him, my knees weakened. Or that my heart picked up speed.

And then his question about my dad came back to me and suddenly, all I wanted was for him to know everything about me. Even though it scared me, there was a part of my soul that wanted to connect with him on that level.

"My dad started collecting cars when my mom passed away." The words were out before I could even stop them. Suddenly, worry choked my throat and I wanted to run from the room. For all I knew, Lucas would take that information and hurt me with it.

He turned to study me. Seconds ticked by and he didn't say anything.

Fear. Worry. Panic. All those emotions raced through me, making me want to throw up. Hadn't he been rude to me since the moment I met him? Why was I allowing myself to be vulnerable to him? Tears pricked at my eyes as the realization that I had completely misunderstood everything washed over me.

I was such an idiot. I needed to get out of here.

"I—um..." The walls felt as if they were closing in on me. "I should go get the milk." And never come back.

Just as I passed by him, he grabbed my hand and pulled me back. "Charlotte?" he asked.

I tried to turn around to face him, but I tripped on my clumsy feet and before I could catch myself, I was falling into him. His two arms wrapped around me and pulled me to his chest.

My heart hammered against my sternum. I was pretty sure he

could feel it. I mean, I could feel it in my toes. Why did I have to be such a klutz? Who literally falls into the arms of a guy?

Only me.

"Charlotte," he said again, this time, softer.

I pinched my lips together and glanced up at him. "Yeah?" Why wasn't he letting me go? Did he like this as much as I was trying to tell myself that I didn't?

He peered down at me and there was an expression on his face that I couldn't quite read. Was it worry? Concern?

Did he think that our relationship had changed because I'd decided to try to connect with him on an emotional level, and now had forced him to have unwanted physical contact with him?

Probably.

The last thing he wanted was for people in Sweet Water to get attached to him. And I had to be the fool that allowed herself to open up to him.

"I'm sorry," I whispered. If I could take the words back, I would.

He brought up his hand and hesitated. Then, he reached out and brushed my hair from my cheek. His gaze met mine and I was pretty sure the entire world around us stopped. Actually, I was pretty sure it stopped everywhere.

"Why are you sorry?" he asked, as he inched his face closer to mine.

Wait. What?

I stood there, like a deer in headlights. What was I supposed to do? Move closer to him? Was that what he wanted?

"You didn't ask me about my mom. I didn't mean to get emotional on you."

He furrowed his brow as he studied me. "That's a silly thing to feel sorry for."

So he wanted to be close to me? Was that what he was saying?

"It is?"

Just as he nodded his response, his phone buzzed. I glanced

around until I realized it was coming from his pocket. He pulled back and glanced down and then back up to me.

"Do you need to get that?" If anything, I was grateful for this interruption. I was pretty sure if our interaction continued, I might do something stupid and forever mar our relationship—or acquaintance. Whatever it was that we had.

The buzzing stopped for a moment and just when I thought we were going to return to where we had been before we were interrupted, the phone buzzed again.

"Yeah. I should get that."

He pulled away and grabbed his phone, his expression hardened as he studied the screen. It was like a completely different person emerged before my eyes. His shoulders tightened and his jaw set. Before I knew it, he walked out of the kitchen and out into the shop.

Now alone, I let out my breath and leaned against the counter. So many emotions were rushing through me and I didn't know what any of them meant.

Or what I wanted them to mean.

CHAPTER ELEVEN

*I*f I thought that things would return to normal when Lucas came back inside, I would have been disappointed. Or, maybe I just needed a reminder of what normal was between Lucas and I really was.

In all actuality, he had been normal. Cold. Distant. Acting as if I didn't exist. That was the normal Lucas I knew and that was what returned when he made his way into the kitchen after his phone call.

There were a few times that I wanted to ask him what was wrong, but from his set jaw and don't-mess-with-me look, I kept quiet.

It didn't take long for the dough to get mixed and placed in the proofer. I kept to one side of the kitchen and Lucas stayed on the other side. Thankfully, I had some ridiculous game on my phone that Drew had downloaded to keep me entertained.

Right before the timer rang, indicating that the rolls had risen enough, Winny came down the stairs looking much more refreshed. I could still see the sleep in her eyes, but the stress lines on her face had lessened.

"I'm so sorry. I think I over slept."

I glanced over to see the time. Two in the morning. Wow. Exhaustion washed over me, bringing me to a yawn. "Yeah, I should probably get home and get some sleep," I said as I untied my apron and made my way over to the hook to hang it.

"Why don't you just sleep here?" Winny asked.

I almost choked on—nothing, as I digested her words. Sleep here? Where Lucas was? Um, no.

I gave her a smile and shook my head. "I should really get home. Dad's going to be wondering where I am and I'm singing in the choir at church tomorrow. Can't really wear this," I said, pulling at my shirt that was covered in flour.

Winny chuckled as she nodded. "I understand. But, I can't let you ride around town in the dark. Lucas, take Charlotte home."

I stepped forward, hoping to stop her from talking. There was no way I could let Lucas give me ride home again. Not when I was so confused. The last thing I needed was to be in a confined space with him.

"I'll be okay. I know the way home like the back of my hand." I could feel Lucas' gaze on me but I refused to glance over at him.

"Charlotte, it's just a ride. I can't let you go without someone with you." She placed her hands on her hips and studied me. "So it's either go with Lucas or sleep here." She raised her eyebrows.

I clenched my jaw, fighting the urge to argue. Then, realizing that there was no way I was going to be able to win this argument, I sighed. "Fine." I turned to face him. "Let's go."

Winny threw her keys over to him and he caught them in one swift movement. It annoyed me that he was so alert this early in the morning.

I didn't wait to see if he was following me. Instead, I made my way out of the bakery and over to Winny's car where I pulled open the passenger door and climbed in.

Part of me hoped that he would tell Winny that there was no way he could take me home so I'd be able to ride my bike. But, moments later, he emerged from the back door and made his way over to the driver's side.

I let out my breath as I folded my arms. Maybe it was because I was angry. Or maybe it was because folding my arms over my chest was a protective move. Like, if there was a barrier between us, he couldn't hurt me.

I was such an idiot.

Why did I let him hurt me like this?

Lucas started the engine and put the car in reverse. When he pulled onto Parsons Street, he glanced over at me.

"Are you mad at me?" he asked.

I honestly didn't think that he wanted to talk to me and when he did, I wasn't sure how to respond. It took my brain a few moments to process what he'd said.

"I—um…" I cleared my throat and turned my attention toward the outside of the car, hoping to gather my thoughts. One sentence kept repeating around in my mind over and over again. I sighed as I fiddled with the hem of my overalls. "You were right," I said.

He paused at a stop sign and looked at me. "I was?"

I nodded and, gathering my courage, I turned to him. "We're from two different worlds. There's really no reason for us to try and force a friendship that's not going to work out." Or a deeper relationship that my heart seemed to think it wanted.

His eyebrows went up and I could see the defense in his eyes.

Desperate to hold my ground, I continued. "It's ridiculous to think we could be anything more than we are." I gave him a small smile, hoping that he would see that I was totally okay with what I was saying, even though I was so totally not.

"More than we are," he repeated slowly.

"Yeah, you know. Acquaintances." I motioned my hand between us.

"Acquaintances," he repeated again.

This was the strangest conversation I'd ever had. I mean, I

used to play parrot with Drew just to annoy him, but I doubted that was what Lucas was doing. It was like he was trying to process what I was saying.

Why was this such a shock to him? It wasn't like he wanted something more.

Right?

"Listen, school is going to start and you'll be part of a different world than I am. It's okay. I'm not hurt." I added.

He glanced over at me again with his eyebrows knit together. "Charlotte, I'm not sure what you are saying."

I sighed, not sure how what I had said was confusing. I was letting him off the hook. He didn't need to feel like he had to be friends with me. "I'm sure when schools starts, you'll find lots of friends. There's no need to force something that's just not going to happen."

He slowed in front of my house and turned to study me. "Are you breaking up with me?"

His question threw me so off guard that I inhaled too sharply and the saliva in my mouth threw me into a coughing fit. I waved away his concern as I covered my mouth and forced myself to calm down. I was exhausted and confused. I just needed to stop talking before I dug myself in too deep.

"Break up? No. Just, releasing you from responsibility," I finally said, my voice coming out wheezy. My eyes were watering and I reached up to dab them.

"Responsibility of being your friend?"

Man, when he repeated what I said, it made me sound like an idiot. Why did I put so much meaning on everything? I'm sure he was just sitting around, thinking we were just acquaintances and here I was, categorizing us.

"You know, forget I said anything," I said, reaching out and grabbing the door handle.

Lucas still looked confused but he nodded. "Okay."

I smiled and pulled the door open and just as I stepped out, his voice made me pause.

"Do you not want to be my...friend?"

I hesitated, not sure what to say to that. That was not what I wanted at all, but I was a realist. I knew what would happen between us once school started. He would soon realize that Sweet Water had a lot more to offer than a broken and confused girl with a dead mom.

And I didn't want to be in this relationship too deep when that realization came.

"I'm just saying, let's be honest with each other. There's nothing about this"—I waved between the two of us—"that makes sense." I gave him a quick smile and stepped out of the car.

Before he answered, I slammed the door and turned, wrapping my arms around my chest and quickening my pace as I made my way up to the front door and opened it.

Once inside, I shut the door just as a sob escaped my lips. I was exhausted and a little bit heart broken.

Which was ridiculous. Lucas wasn't mine.

I was the stupid girl who had interpreted everything wrong. Lucas didn't have feelings for me. Why would he? I was so broken, that I was pretty sure that all the king's men and all the king's horses could never put me together again.

That was the last thing Lucas needed. The mess that was my life.

I slipped off my shoes and made my way upstairs to my room. I didn't even undress as I slipped under the covers and pulled them over my head.

I angrily wiped the tears from my cheeks and I blew out my breath. Tomorrow I was going to be stronger. I had to be. There as no other option.

Tomorrow I would stop caring about Lucas.

And just as my mind slipped into the calmness of sleep, 'yeah, right' floated through my mind.

Crap.

"Cannon ball!"

My eyes whipped open as my whole body tensed. Through my hazy morning eyes, I barely braced myself enough before all seventy-five pounds of my brother came hurtling at me.

I yelped and rolled, but not in enough time to protect my body. He landed on me, smashing me into the mattress and comforter.

"Wake up," he said, sticking his face inches from mine.

I groaned, fighting off the slur of words that I wanted to say. Some were not so nice and would require some forgiveness today at church. So I bit them back.

"What is the matter with you?" I said, pushing on him with my free arm.

He shrugged, bounced a few times, and then climbed off me. "Dad said to come wake you up."

I rolled my eyes, grabbed my glasses, and sighed. If I didn't hurry, I'd be late for choir practice. It was something my mom and I used to do every Sunday and even though I went alone now, I couldn't bring myself to stop going.

I ushered Drew out of my room and shut the door. After a quick shower, I got dressed in my pale yellow dress that Mom and I bought last summer for my Uncle Pat's wedding, and attempted to apply some makeup. I wasn't a pro by any means but I did try to look good for church.

After I quickly blow-dried my hair, I grabbed my shoes and purse and headed downstairs.

Just as I neared the bottom, I heard a familiar voice.

Lucas.

My stomach knotted and my heart hammered in my chest.

Why was he here?

I peeked around the corner and my body went numb.

And...why, oh why, did he have to look so incredibly good, standing in my kitchen in a suit and tie?

"Lottie," Dad said, waving me into the kitchen.

Well, there went my exit strategy. Dad saw me, which meant I wasn't leaving, which meant, I was going to have to be in the same room with Lucas.

"Hey, Dad," I said, stepping past Lucas. I tried not to notice but I could physically feel his gaze on me as I made my way over to the sink to pour a glass of water.

"Hey, Charlotte," Lucas said. His voice was soft. Quiet.

I nodded in his direction as I busied myself with drinking.

"Lucas was just telling me about your baking rescue last night." Dad waited until I set the glass down before he clapped me on the back. "I'm sure Pastor Bryant will be grateful for your hard work."

I nodded at Dad, and then to Lucas. "Yeah. Winny was tired and I was happy to help." I then nodded to the both of them. "I should go. I'm late for choir." Just as I pulled open the back door to head outside, realization dawned on me. I'd left my bike at Winny's.

"That's why Lucas is here." Dad's voice brought me to a stop. I turned slowly to see that Lucas' hands were shoved into the front of his pockets and he was studying me.

What was he doing?

"I'm sorry, what?" I tucked my hair behind my ear. My hands felt clammy from my nerves, which were firing throughout my whole body.

"Winny insisted that I join the choir as well and since you left your bike at the bakery, I thought I'd pick you up."

I stared at Lucas. Hadn't I told him yesterday that I didn't want to this? That he didn't need to try to be my friend? He was released from any responsibility.

"I'm fine. I can get there on my own." I pulled my purse strap up higher on my shoulder. I'd walk there in the early morning heat if I had to. I really didn't want to get into his car. Or be close to him at all.

Lucas swallowed and nodded. "I know you can. I, um..." He

moved his gaze to Dad who was studying me. "I was just dropping something off to your dad. I'll go." A polite smile appeared as he ducked his head and moved toward our front door.

"Hang on, son," Dad called out. Lucas paused with his hand on the doorknob.

Dad took his time turning to study me. "What's the matter with you?" he asked with his voice low.

I shrugged as I shifted to fiddle with a fraying piece of wallpaper. "I can get to church on my own."

Dad snorted. "He is being nice. Have you forgotten your manners?"

I sighed and faced Dad. "You don't understand. We're...he's..." Words weren't forming in my mind. I wanted to say something. Come up with a great excuse as to why Lucas couldn't give me a ride to church. But Dad would never understand.

Dad's eyebrows remained raised as if he were waiting for me to come up with a good excuse. When one didn't come, his jaw muscle clenched and he nodded toward Lucas. "Say thank you to the boy who is taking you."

I glared at him and then nodded. "Sure, Lucas, I'd love a ride."

Lucas turned and looked unsure, so I shot him a big smile. That seemed to appease him enough to nod and pull open the door.

"See you at church," Dad said as he waved at us.

Lucas nodded as he held the door open for me. I tried not to react to his presence when I walked past him, but that was a joke. He smelled like sandalwood and the beach and I could feel the nearness of his chest. My heart pounded at a dangerous pace and I swallowed as hard as I could to push down the feelings that were running like horses on a beach.

If I didn't get my body under control, I was going to be a goner. There would be no coming back from Lucas Addington.

CHAPTER TWELVE

The ride to church was quiet. I kept my gaze outside and my body turned away from Lucas. I needed as much distance as I could put between us if I was going to keep myself protected.

"I'm sorry."

Lucas' soft voice pulled my attention over to him. Maybe it was because I didn't expect him to care enough to say anything to me. I'm sure Winny forced him to pick me up. I furrowed my brow as I allowed my gaze to roam across his face.

"For what?" I spilled out before I could stop it.

He looked sideways at me for a moment before returning his eyes to the road. "For over stepping. You know, picking you up." He sighed as he shifted on his seat. His hands squeezed and released the steering wheel a few times.

I let out my breath slowly, cursing myself for making such a big deal out of nothing. If showing Lucas that I didn't care about him was my goal, I was failing miserably at it. He could clearly tell that I was having a reaction to him. And the only reason I was having a reaction to him was because I cared.

Great. Stealthy, I was not.

"It's okay. I was just shocked to see you in my kitchen, that's all." I gave him a small smile.

He studied me for a moment before turning left on Main. "You sure that's all?"

I nodded. "Of course. We can be acquaintances who pick each other up. You can be my taxi."

He pinched his lips together and I could see him focus on my words. "Okay. If that's what you want."

"Sure."

He pulled into the church parking lot and turned off the engine. "Although, we'll be seeing a lot more of each other now," he said, turning to face me.

I furrowed my brow. "What?"

He fiddled with his key chain. "Well, we see each other at the bakery and now, at your house." He gave me a sly smile and pulled on his door handle.

My brain finally caught up with my words. "What? How?" Was he moving into our house? Why?

I scrambled to pull on my door handle and dash around the hood of the car before he slipped into the church. I grabbed onto his elbow to stop him. Of course, my thoughts got all scrambled because as soon as I touched him, the only thought that remained was how incredibly buff he was.

But, eventually I pushed that out of my mind and focused. "Where else am I going to be seeing you?" I squinted as I stared up at him.

He leaned close to me and I became very away of how close our faces were to each other. It would have taken just a few centimeters to press my lips to his. And I became overwhelmed with the desire to do just that.

"I guess you'll just have to wait to find out." He leaned closer with each word and my breath hitched in my throat.

I was pretty certain he was going to kiss me. At least, that was what every romance movie I'd ever seen had taught me. My eyes widened as I took in the gold flecks in his eyes. They contrasted against the dark, chocolate brown coloring.

He had a look in them that told me, he was fighting something. I wanted to think that it was the pull he felt between liking me, and not, because it was that exact pull I was feeling for him inside of my chest.

His eyes flicked down to my lips and I was pretty sure I was going to collapse right there, in the church parking lot.

"I'm a lot more than just the rich kid you've categorized me as," he said. His voice was low and gravely and sent shivers down my spine.

All I could do was nod. I was too afraid of what my voice would sound like if I spoke.

He studied me for a moment longer before straightening and adjusting his suit coat. After a second glance in my direction, he turned and climbed up the stairs to the church doors and disappeared inside.

I took a deep breath as I tucked my hair behind my ears and gathered my bearings. What the heck had that just been? Why did I turn into a bumbling idiot when I was around him? And why, oh why, did I feel so disappointed that he hadn't kissed me?

I swallowed as I grabbed onto my purse strap and headed up the stairs after him. At least at church, I didn't have to talk to him. And for the rest of the day, because I didn't work at Winny's. I had a whole day before I had to face Lucas again and right now, I needed every minute I could get.

———

Thankfully, I went through the entire choir practice and church service without having to talk to Lucas. Even though my gaze, unintentionally, kept slipping over to him, that was all the interaction we had. Which was good. I wasn't sure I could handle much more.

Dad was waiting by the car after the luncheon when I walked up with Drew in tow. I wanted to get out of there before the after-service lingering happened and I found myself face to face with Lucas. Again.

"Ready?" Dad asked as I pulled open the passenger door at the same time Drew pulled open the back seat door.

I nodded and climbed in. "More than you know," I said, as I buckled.

Dad started up the car and pulled out of the parking lot. Just as he straightened out the car, Lucas appeared next to Dad's window.

I wanted to tell Dad to keep driving, but of course, he lingered there and rolled his window down.

"Hey, Lucas," Dad said.

Lucas leaned down and nodded. "Hey, Mr. Robinson."

"Coming over later?"

Lucas' eyes flickered to me and then quickly back to Dad. I was pretty sure he saw my jaw drop. "That's the plan. I'm going to make sure Winny gets home and then I'll head over."

Dad patted the car door as he nodded. "Awesome. I can't wait to get started on the car."

Lucas smiled. "Me neither."

They said goodbye and Dad drove off. I stared at him, trying to figure out what had just happened.

"What…what's happening?" I finally managed.

Dad glanced at me as he pulled onto Main. "What are you talking about?"

I scoffed. "Lucas? What are you doing?"

Dad settled back as he drove down the road. "I thought you liked Lucas."

Ugh. There was too much confusion in that one little phrase. "I do not *like* Lucas."

Dad looked confused as he studied me. "You don't like Lucas?"

From the look on Dad's face, he hadn't meant the type of like that had come to my mind. Man, I was a mess. "I mean, yeah, he's okay. But, why does he have to come over?"

"Charlotte, he's a customer. I can't just kick him out. He bought the Chevy. We're going to work on it together to get it up and running." Dad looked at me. "I figured you be grateful for that. You were so excited when I told you I sold it."

I groaned and folded my arms. Now there was a tug of war going on inside me. One that said I wanted this car out of our yard as soon as possible. The other part wasn't sure having Lucas over here on my days off was the answer.

"But...can't you..." Words just weren't forming in my mind. Instead, I just leaned back and sighed.

Dad reached over and patted my knee. "You'll survive. I'm sure of it. And who knows, spending time with him might help you change your impression of him."

I nodded as I focused outside the window. That was not what the problem was. I was rapidly hating the fact that I couldn't seem to hate Lucas anymore. There was so much more safety in pain and hurt. When you let go of that, you were vulnerable. And I was pretty sure being vulnerable with Lucas was not something that would keep me safe.

"Okay, Dad," I said as he pulled into our driveway and shut off the engine. The last thing I wanted was for us to keep talking about this and for him to let things slip to Lucas.

I pulled open my door and crossed the yard. Once inside, I headed upstairs where I closed my bedroom door and flopped down on my bed.

As I lay there, halfway covered by my down comforter, I stared up at the ceiling and took a deep breath. I was pretty sure that I was making a bigger deal of what was happening between me and Lucas. I mean, it wasn't like I had deep, meaningful feelings for him.

I was just confused. He confused me.

It really was Mom's fault. Ever since her death, I'd been this emotional basket-case and I was more influenced by people in my life than before. Lucas was the first person that had entered my life since Mom, so of course I was going to have these confusing feelings for a complete stranger.

Groaning, I covered my face with my arm and closed my eyes. Maybe if I fell asleep I would wake up from this nightmare and Mom would be here and I wouldn't be so confused.

If only...

———

I woke up two hours later with a crick in my neck. I winced as I sat up. After twisting a few times to loosen my back, I glanced out the window. The sun was shining into my room, warming the air around it.

I reached up and pulled my hair into a messy bun at the nape of my neck. After I changed out of my dress and into a pair of fraying overall shorts and white tee, I made my way out of my room.

Just as I neared the stairs, my phone rang, vibrating in my pocket. I pulled it out and glanced down.

Maddie.

"Hey," I said as I brought the phone to my ear.

"Where have you been? I've been calling you for like the last hour."

I shrugged but then realized she couldn't see it. "I was at church and then took a nap." I padded down the stairs and into the kitchen where I grabbed an apple. "What's up?"

She sighed heavily into the phone. An indicator that she was about to enter into a very long story. "Lucas stopped by The Bean."

My heart picked up speed. Dumb, stupid heart. I cleared my throat, nervous that she could hear it. "Oh yeah?"

"Yes. Why didn't you tell me that he purchased a car from your dad?"

I sighed, instantly knowing where this conversation was going. "Um, I literally just found out like two hours ago."

Maddie remained quiet as if she were mulling my words around in her mind. "Well, since you are my best friend and I'm pretty sure Lucas and I are soul mates, I'm coming over as soon as my shift is over."

I had just taken a big bite of my apple and as soon as she said the words, I inhaled, causing apple juice to shoot to the back of my throat but there wasn't time to cough it out. I needed to stop what was happening. "I'm—you're—"

I eventually had to give up trying to talk until my coughing fit died down. My eyes were watering and my throat felt raw, but I was no longer coughing like a maniac. "You want to come over here?" I rasped.

"Um hum," she said followed by a "What was that?"

"Apple juice," I said as I walked over to the sink and grabbed out a glass from the cupboard and filled it with water. After I took a long drink, I set it back into the sink and focused on what my best friend was saying.

"So, you're cool with me coming over tonight?"

No. I wasn't. But there was no way I could say that to my best friend. Especially when she wanted Lucas and I didn't.

"Yeah, okay."

"Good."

I could literally hear the joy in her voice. Was it wrong that it made my stomach twist?

"Alright, I should probably go find my dad. I'll see you when you get off work," I said.

"You're a doll," she said in a sing-song voice. "You are really an amazing best friend." Her voice became serious and made me want to vomit.

No I wasn't. I wasn't a good friend at all. I was trying really hard not to crush on the guy she wanted to date. I was the worst.

"Okay," I said in a whisper as she continued the conversation about how excited she was and how long work was going to seem now that she had to wait.

I listened, giving her a few courtesy um-hmms. Then, she let me go because her boss was giving her a dirty look. We said good-bye and after I turned my screen off, I set it down next to me and dipped my head.

I was so confused that my head hurt. Maybe I should go back to bed. But, even though that sounded tempting, I couldn't. Maddie was coming over in a few hours which meant Lucas was going to be here sometime between now and then and no matter how much I wanted to tell myself that I didn't really care about that, I knew that wasn't true.

I cared. Maybe a little too much.

CHAPTER THIRTEEN

I distracted myself with a book while I waited. I was getting into the story just as my front door opened and I heard Lucas' voice carry inside. I tried not to squirm as I adjusted my position on the armchair in the front room, all the while, staring at the book in front of me.

None of this was fair. I wanted so badly not to have any feelings for Lucas but my head and body didn't seem to want to listen because as soon as I saw him step into the house, my heart took off galloping.

I swallowed as I stared hard at the words, trying to figure out what they were saying. How did I forget how to read in ten seconds flat?

"Hey, Charlotte." Lucas' voice made my stomach lighten and my whole body heat up.

"Hey," I managed as I raised my hand in his direction. And then I felt like an idiot. What was my problem?

"I'll grab us some water and then we can get started," Dad said.

Oh, right. Dad was in the room. I hadn't even noticed.

"Sure, Mr. Robinson."

I kept my gaze on my book, but every one of my senses was

focused on Lucas and what he was doing. First, he fidgeted a bit. Then he wandered over to look at a few photos on the wall. And then, he walked over to me.

"What are you reading?" he asked, dipping down to study the front of my book.

I shrugged as I slammed the book closed and tucked it next to me. "It was my mom's." In truth, it was one of those cheesy romances that made me sigh. For some reason, I didn't want Lucas to know that I actually enjoyed reading them.

His eyebrows were raised as he stepped back. "Sorry," he muttered.

Regret flooded my body as the tone of my voice and the meaning behind shutting the book and hiding it raced through my mind. Not wanting to hurt him became priority one. "I mean, my mom liked to read this one," I said, grabbing the book and holding it up for him to see.

Wow. I seriously changed moods faster than a NASCAR racer shifted gears.

He studied the cover and then glanced over at me. I could see there were questions he wanted to ask and I wasn't sure if I wanted him to do that.

Thankfully, Dad walked in with two water bottles and handed one to Lucas who thanked him as he took it. Dad told him they should get started and just as quickly as Lucas had come in, he was gone.

As the front door shut behind them, I let out the breath I'd been holding, grateful that I'd managed to hold it together while he was here. I was in some serious trouble if I didn't get my feelings under control.

I scooted down on the chair until my feet were resting on the coffee table and I was able to rest my book on my chest as I read.

An hour ticked by before the door opened and I pulled my attention up from my book. Maddie's voice carried into the room and I forced my beating heart to calm down.

It wasn't Lucas, body. Get a grip.

Maddie giggled something incoherent and then appeared in the foyer.

"Char," she said as she shut the door and gave me a wide smile.

I closed my book, adjusted my glasses, and sat up. "Hey, Mads." I set the book on the coffee table and stood.

She half-walked, half-glided into the room. I swear, I thought she was going to break out into song.

"How can you be in here with a book while sexy things are going on outside?"

I gave her a look that I hoped told her I wasn't amused. "Ugh, Maddie. That's my dad." Make a joke of it. That seemed like the best course of action.

Her smiled faltered and then she smacked my arm. "I wasn't talking about your dad." Then a dreamy look crossed over her face that made me want to throw up. "Lucas," she whispered as she fanned her face.

I tried not to roll my eyes. I also had to try really hard not to deck her. Neither of which were fair to her. It wasn't her fault I had so many issues. It also wasn't her fault that I couldn't decide what I wanted in terms of Lucas. She lived an uncomplicated life. I didn't. Who was I to stop her from being happy? Even if there was a rock in the pit of my stomach from the thought of her being happy *with Lucas*.

She flopped down on the couch and began to twirl her hair around her finger as she studied me. "So, what do you want to do?"

I shrugged as I sat back down on the armchair I had just vacated. "We could watch TV. Go to the beach." I glanced over at her to see if she was going to offer any options.

She was nodding, and when I was no longer offering opinions, she glanced over at me. "Or we could go outside."

I groaned. I didn't mean to, but it just slipped out. "Seriously, Mads? Isn't that a little obvious?"

She giggled and moved to stand. "Honey, how is he ever going to know that I'm interested if I don't show it?"

I swallowed, realizing that there was really no way I was going to get out of this. She was here to see Lucas and nothing was going to stand in her way. Nothing.

Which meant, I was going to see Lucas. With Maddie. Great.

"I'm more about staying inside where there's air conditioning." I offered.

"What a perfect idea. Let's get in our bikinis and tan outside." She pulled off her shirt, exposing her polkadot bikini underneath.

I so desperately wanted to back track, but I wasn't Superman. I couldn't fly super fast around the Earth to turn back time. When Maddie got an idea in her head, watch out. There was no stopping her.

Which meant there was really no way I was going to get out of this.

"Mads," I said, attempting to stand up for myself.

"Come on, Charlotte. I can't do this by myself." She pushed out her bottom lip and stared at me. "I'd do it for you."

That was true. She may be scatter-brained and a little demanding, but she was loyal to a fault. So I groaned and headed for my room. "You owe me big time," I called down. I doubt she heard me through her cheering.

After I dressed in my black swimsuit, I grabbed a towel and slipped a coverall over my suit and headed down the stairs. Maddie was still in just her shorts and bikini top and I couldn't help but compare the two of us.

Where she was endowed, I was seriously lacking. I had grapes compared to her. But, she grabbed my hand and dragged me outside before I could slip upstairs and hide under my covers.

Dad and Lucas were by the Chevy. As we walked past, Lucas paused, glancing over at me, my skin heated from his gaze. I swallowed hard, my throat becoming dry.

"Hey, Lucas," Maddie said, practically sauntering past him.

"Where are you ladies off to?" Lucas asked. I couldn't help but notice that his gaze remained on me—not Maddie.

Heat flushed my cheeks as I dropped my gaze.

"To do some tanning."

Dad rolled out from under the car. "Sunscreen, peanut."

I tried not to glare at him as I nodded. "Of course." Ever since Mom, Dad's overprotective tendencies were in full force—when he remembered.

"I'll take care of her, Mr. Robinson," Maddie said, wrapping her arm around my shoulders.

An awkward feeling settled in the air and I moved my gaze from Maddie, back over to Lucas. He was watching us with a hard-to-read expression on his face. What was he thinking?

"Well, you guys look busy, we won't bother you anymore," Maddie said as she tugged on me and I almost fell over my feet.

"Whoa," Lucas said and suddenly his hand was wrapped around my arm. How had he gotten over to me so fast?

Maybe *he* was Superman.

"Oh, Char. She's such a klutz. Come on," she said, motioning toward one of the only patches of grass left in our yard.

I glanced down at Lucas' hand, which was still touching me. Why hadn't he let me go?

"You okay?" he asked. There was a soft tone to his voice. Like he...cared.

I nodded as I stepped toward Maddie, effectively breaking the connection we had.

"Wrench," Dad called from under the car.

That seemed to snap Lucas out of his trance and he nodded and turned.

I took that opportunity to move as fast as I could away from the car. Maddie took longer to make her way over to the grass and lay down. Once she was situated, she glanced over at me.

I'd busied myself with rubbing sunscreen on my arms. I was still in my swim suit cover while she was down to her bikini. Ugh.

She looked like a glamorous Greek goddess. Me? I looked like a white sheet with too much fabric softener dumped over it.

Eventually, all the sunscreen was absorbed, so I leaned back on my elbow and tipped my face toward the sky. The warm rays washed over my skin and for a moment, I began to relax. Maybe coming out here and braving skin cancer was worth it. If anything, I was probably dangerously low on vitamin D and my body knew it.

"Ugh, why do you have so many ridiculous cars in your yard?" Maddie's voice drew my attention over to her.

I glanced in the direction she was glaring to see a VW bug. Its blue paint had faded severely from the sun. "It's never bothered you before," I said, sitting up and wrapping my arms around my knees.

She propped herself up on an elbow and peered at me from over her sunglasses. "Well, that's because it's never blocked a guy's view before. I mean, how's he going to appreciate me when he can't even see me?"

I looked toward the driveway—in the direction of Lucas and my dad. My stomach did a little flip at the thought of his being on the other side. Was he thinking about me too? Was he just as frustrated with the lack of sight?

And then I shook my head. Not hard enough to be obvious, but enough to shake that stupid thought from my mind.

"He's never going to figure out we're destined to be together if he doesn't see me," Maddie huffed.

"He's not like that," tumbled from my lips. I pinched them shut when I realized that I had just spoken.

Maddie slipped her glasses off so she could stare at me. "What?"

Heat pricked my cheeks as I reached out to fiddle with a few blades of grass. "Nothing," I mumbled. This was not the conversation I wanted to have. Besides, why was I defending Lucas to her?

"If you know something about the guy I like, it's a best friend's duty to tell her best friend."

Ooh, Maddie was good. Challenging my best friend status. If I was truly her best friend, then she's right, it was my duty to tell her about the guy she liked. I wouldn't be fantasying about Lucas. Wondering what it would be like to kiss him. I would step back. Allow her to pursue him.

"Char," Maddie said, taking time to sound out every syllable of my name.

I glanced over at her and sighed. "It's just that Lucas is a lot deeper than just some good looking guy"—Maddie raised her eyebrows and the desire to backtrack took over—"I mean, what other people think is good looking. I don't think he's good looking." I let out my breath in a whoosh. What was I doing? I needed to stop talking.

Maddie got a far-off look in her eyes, which I took as a good sign. Perhaps, if I just kept talking about Lucas and her, then she'd ignore the fact that I was pretty sure my skin was so hot, it was going to set on fire.

"So he's like a Mr. Darcy." The smile that tugged on her lips made me want to punch her, which was a strange sensation. I mean, I loved Maddie. She was like my sister. I wasn't supposed to get angry when she daydreamed about a guy that wasn't mine.

When she glanced over at me, I realized that I was supposed to respond so I just nodded. "Sure. Yeah, Mr. Darcy." What was supposed to come out as a joking response, actually had some seriousness behind it. Lucas was a lot like Mr. Darcy now that I thought about it. He was rich, came across as a jerk at first, but then had so much hidden up his sleeve that when it came out, it hit you over the head.

Maddie stretched out, tipping her face toward the sky. "I like it. He can be Darcy and I'll be his Elizabeth."

Suddenly feeling sick, I shifted against the ground and stood. "I, um, need some water. I'll be back," I said as I made my way into the house, leaving my swimsuit cover and everything else on the grass next to Maddie.

Right now, I didn't care. The only thing I could think about was getting away from Maddie and her obsession with Lucas. I needed a tall glass of water and a break from her crush before I did or said something I would regret.

Because if I did that, I'm not sure I could ever come back from it.

CHAPTER FOURTEEN

The cold, air-conditioned air surrounded me as I shut the front door and leaned against it. My heart was racing and my mind swarming as I kept replaying our conversation over and over in mind.

What was wrong with me? When had I become this crazy, jealous friend? It was so not me and right now, I needed to get a handle on it before I reacted, forever marring my relationship with quite a few people.

After taking a few deep breaths, I pushed off the door and made my way into the kitchen where I got a glass down from the cupboard and turned on the faucet. Cool water rushed across my fingers as I stared out the window.

What was I going to do? Did the feelings I had burning in my chest mean what I thought they did? Did I...like Lucas? Was it possible?

I wanted to lie to myself and tell myself that I was crazy. That he'd somehow wiggled his way into my thoughts, turning me into a delusional, emotional wreck. But I knew that wasn't the case.

No, from the hot emotions that were flowing through me right now, I knew it only meant one thing.

I had feelings for Lucas. Deep and ridiculous feelings, for the obnoxious boy who had spilled his coffee on me and made me so unbelievably angry.

Man, I was in trouble.

The back door slammed, causing me to jump. I turned, half expecting to see Dad or Drew, but instead, I was met with Lucas' warm, brown eyes. His gaze ran over my body and I swear, I saw his cheeks turn pink as he brought his gaze up to meet mine.

That's when I realized I was standing in the middle of my kitchen in just my swimsuit. Sure, he'd seen me in it before, but now? I felt exposed and enormously self-conscious.

"Hey," I said, reaching for a dish towel and trying to inconspicuously cover my body with it.

He studied me for a moment before he made his way over to the sink and stood just a few inches away from me. "How's tanning?" he asked, reaching up and opening a cupboard. When he discovered only spices, he went to the next one.

Not wanting him to spend another second in the house with me, I leaned forward and pulled open the cupboard with the glasses. He must have zeroed in on that exact one because suddenly, I was a breath away from him.

He paused, turning to me. It was like everything in the room slowed. All that I could see or feel was him. My heart pounded so hard, I could hear it in my ears. His gaze met mine and then for a second, flicked down to my lips just to return up to my gaze. It happened so fast that I doubted even seeing it.

"Charlotte," he said, his voice so low that it made my toes tingle. Like there was something he wanted to tell me.

I felt frozen. I couldn't move. Every muscle had come to a screeching halt. I wanted to bolt. I wanted to tell him that he was crazy to think of me like that. That I was the last person he should want to be with.

"Glasses are here," I said, clearing my throat and stepping back.

I needed the space. If I didn't leave right now, I wasn't sure all the self-control in the world would keep me from him.

"How long does it take to get a glass of water?" Maddie's voice filled the air making me jump higher than I thought humanly possible.

Lucas glanced back at her before turning to the sink and flipping the water on. He looked so casual, like nothing had just happened between us. I, on the other hand, felt like I was having a heart attack. My heart was hammering and every part of my body was sweating. All I could think about was the fact that I could have just kissed Lucas and my best friend might have seen.

I was the worst person in the world. If there was a prize for crappiest best friend, you might as well hand it over to me now. I couldn't imagine anyone else winning that.

"Yep. Just helping Lucas with his glass," I said, wincing at the strained and high-pitched way my voice came out. I pinched my lips together. Probably best to just not speak anymore.

Maddie furrowed her brow as she studied me, and then Lucas. Then she nodded slowly. "Well, great. I was getting kind of lonely outside."

I smiled as I grabbed her arm and linked mine through it. I needed space so the quicker I got her out of the kitchen the better. "Let's go. I've got my back to work on."

Maddie started to protest—I knew what she was doing—but I couldn't be her wingman. Not right now. And probably not ever if being her wingman helped her win Lucas. I was pretty sure my heart might break if I had to watch that.

And thinking that thought made the pit in my stomach grow bigger. I should be happy for her right now. I should help her win the guy she was convinced was the right person for her. But I couldn't. That made me selfish but right now, I needed to be selfish if I wanted to survive.

When we got outside, I flopped onto my towel, wishing I could bury my face into the ground—if only it wasn't so hard. Instead, I rested my forehead against the grass and let out my breath.

When Maddie didn't say anything, I glanced to the side to see her watching me. Regret and worry filled my stomach as I pushed myself to sitting and smiled over at her.

"What?" I asked, grateful that my voice had managed to return to normal.

Maddie just studied me. I could tell that she was mulling some thoughts around in her mind, trying to figure out the best way to approach me. I hated that I'd betrayed my best friend. I should know better than to fall for the guy she liked.

"Do you like Lucas?"

Her directness hit me so hard that all my breath whooshed from my chest. I coughed a few times, hoping I looked relaxed and not like the wreck that I felt. I knew what I was about to say was a blatant lie, but I had every intention of making the words the truth, once I got my heart to stop reacting to Lucas every time he walked into the room or looked at me.

I just needed self-control and I knew that at some point, I was going to have it. I just needed time.

"I don't like Lucas. In fact, I can't stand him. He is just every-where I am. He's like a summer cold I can't shake." I steadied my gaze even though my stomach was in knots. I hated that I was even saying these words about him. From what I had learned, Lucas was a really nice person. He put up walls but inside, he was good. Oh...so good.

And I was the idiot who let herself fall for him.

Maddie furrowed her brow as she studied me. Then she sighed, nodding as she adjusted her legs so they were no longer tucked underneath her, but stretched out in front. "Well, that's a relief. I was worried, but hearing you say that makes me feel better."

I copied her, running my legs parallel with hers. I was grateful that we were no longer staring at each other. That way, I didn't have to worry about my expressions giving me away.

A throat cleared behind us and I about jumped out of my skin. Turning, I saw Lucas a few feet off. He was carrying two sodas in his hands. From the hardened look on his face, I couldn't quite tell if he'd heard our conversations or not.

Inside, I prayed he'd just walked up. I didn't know what I was going to do if I found out he'd heard what I said.

"Well, aren't you a gentleman," Maddie said, whipping out her gorgeous smile and aiming it right at Lucas who took a step forward.

"Thought you ladies might get thirsty," Lucas said, walking straight over to Maddie and handing a drink to her.

I parted my lips as I watched their interaction. It hurt more than I cared to admit that he didn't even look over at me. But it was like a horror scene—I couldn't pull my gaze away from them.

Maddie took the can from him and I swear, she let her fingers linger a tad longer than necessary next to his. Fury built up inside of me so I ripped my gaze away from them. I couldn't look anymore. I had to stop liking Lucas. Right now.

I wrapped my arms around my knees as I drew them up to my chest. I hugged them as I rested my chin on the top of my legs. I swallowed hard, trying to force down the pain that was rising up inside of me. I'd felt worse pain than this. I could handle it. After all, hadn't that been what I'd been doing since the day Mom died?

Forcing pain to the deep, darkest parts of my body?

Lucas turned, flicking his gaze down to me. I couldn't read his thoughts as he pushed the soda toward me. "Here," he said as he practically dropped it into my lap.

I scrambled to grab it. The cool metal shocked my skin as I held it off to the side. With the way my stomach was churning, the last thing I needed was to put a crap ton of sugar inside of me.

"Hey, Lucas, I was wondering if you were busy tomorrow? I mean, school starts on Tuesday and I have a few supplies still to get. If you're a total dweeb like me and have completely forgotten some pens, maybe we could go together?"

I kept my gaze trained on the ground in front of me as I tried really hard not to listen in on their conversation. Both of them were free. They had every right to go shopping together. What did I care?

I could feel Lucas' gaze on me for a moment before he turned to Maddie. "I've got to work in the afternoon. But maybe after."

Ooo, dagger to the chest. Man, what was wrong with me? How was this *getting over Lucas*?

Maddie giggled, said something about him calling her, and then Lucas left. I slipped my sunglasses on as I laid back on my towel and closed my eyes. Maddie started talking about what she was going to wear the first day of school and I gave her the cursory, um hmms, to appease her.

We spent the next few hours laying in the sun. Thankfully, Lucas didn't make any more appearances, which made my resolve to stop liking him much easier. In fact, by the time Maddie kissed both of my cheeks and declared she had to go, I was feeling much better.

Hopeful, in fact. It was like one of the 60-minute flu epidemics. After the initial wave, everything settles down. I was feeling like an idiot that I'd let my emotions get so muddled up before. I didn't like Lucas. We weren't destined to be together.

I was just confused and hurting. That was all.

Once Maddie pulled away, I lowered my hand from the final wave and turned to make my way back into the house. Dad was standing in the entryway with Drew who was bouncing up and down.

"Calm down, dude," Dad said, laughing as Drew hung on his arm.

"Where are you guys going tonight?" I asked, shutting the door and tying the towel tighter around my waist.

Dad glanced over at me. "We've got some father/son bonding

to do. You don't mind, bug? Staying here so we can have a man's night out?"

I wrinkled my nose as I shook my head and headed over to the fridge. "Sounds smelly and sweaty." I raised both hands. "I'm more than happy to hold the fort down. In fact, there's some chocolate cake in the fridge and a steaming hot bubble bath calling my name." I pulled out the cake and held it up as evidence.

Dad chuckled as he nodded. "Sounds like a real rager. Just keep the noise level down so Mrs. Protresca doesn't call the cops on us."

I saluted him as I made my way upstairs. "It'll be nice to have the house to myself for the night." I'd babysat one too many times since Mom died. Alone actually sounded like heaven.

As I neared the top of the stairs, I swore I heard Dad say something about Lucas, but deciding to stay true to my decision to put him from my mind, I didn't ask what he had said. Instead, I slipped into my bedroom and out of my swimsuit. Once my obnoxiously fluffy robe was tied around me, I padded into the bathroom and turned the water on.

Focusing my thoughts on something other than Lucas was the first step in my twelve-step program to forget Lucas Addington. I was going to be strong. I had to be.

CHAPTER FIFTEEN

*E*nya played softly from my phone as I slipped farther under the massive mound of bubbles above me. The cake was demolished in three seconds flat, its empty container sitting on the floor next to the tub. The lavender smell, mixed with my full stomach, was finally relaxing me.

I closed my eyes and tipped my head back as I let out my breath. My muscles ached from the stress they'd been holding since...well, at least for as long as Mom had been gone. I wiggled my toes over to the faucet where I flipped on the hot. The water warmed as I sunk father into it.

It was final. I was going to live here. There was nothing in the world that would ever get me to leave this bathroom or this warm water. Noise outside the door drew my attention over and I sighed. Well, anything but that. Dad and Drew must be back which meant my break as a single person was over. I sighed as I straightened, grabbing my phone to glance at the time.

Huh. That was strange. They'd only been gone for 45 minutes. Maybe they forgot their keys.

Before I could call out to them, the bathroom door opened. I started to protest, telling Drew that I was in here, but all thought left my mind along with my voice when I found myself staring into the very startled eyes of Lucas.

His eyebrows shot up as his gaze roamed over me and then he clamped his eyes shut as he slapped his hand over his eyes.

Finally, I found my sanity as I twisted onto my side. Bless the overly foaming bubbles. I was almost one hundred percent positive that he saw nothing, but just in case, I wasn't risking it. "What are you doing? Get out!" I gasped as red-hot heat flushed over my body.

This was bad, oh so bad.

Lucas didn't even say anything. Instead, he fumbled around to find the doorknob and then turned it, slipping out into the hall. Once he was safely on the other side of the now closed door, I peeked around just to make sure, then stood, grabbing a towel and drying off faster than those blowers in a carwash.

I slipped on my robe, pulled it closed at the top of my neck, and held everything in place as I stared at myself in the mirror. Why did this keep happening? Why did it have to be Lucas seeing me in compromising situations?

I swear, I thought I was going to die from embarrassment.

A soft knock sounded on the door and I closed my eyes. I wanted to tell him to go away. That I was fine. But I feared how my voice would sound if I spoke, so I decided to keep it brief. "Yes?"

There was a pause. "I, um, didn't see anything. I swear."

I closed my eyes again as frustration and embarrassment closed my throat. It was an honest mistake. I was totally fine. In fact, given enough time, I just might laugh about this.

But standing in the bathroom, dissecting what happened wasn't going to make me or him feel any better. So right now, I just needed to end the conversation and move on.

I reached out, grabbed the door handle and turned it. I took a deep breath as I stepped out into the hall, forcing a calm, almost teasing smile. "I know. I'm fine," I squeaked as I hurried past him and into my room. I didn't look back as I slammed my door and sunk onto my bed.

I waited for a few minutes to see if he would knock on my door, but no sound came. Hoping I'd deterred him, I dressed in a pair of cut-off overalls and a plum t-shirt. Feeling somewhat better now that I was clothed, I took a deep breath and opened the door.

Right on Lucas.

He was leaning on the other side of the hallway with his hands in his pockets and his legs extended. He was studying the ground but then startled up when I opened the door.

He met my gaze and I swear he blushed. Not wanting to focus on that, I decided to speak.

"Is this your new pastime now?" I asked, quirking an eyebrow as I passed him and headed toward the stairs.

The sound of his footsteps behind me caused my shoulders to slump. Why was he following me? Did he want to torture me?

"I really didn't know you were in there. I figured you'd gone out with your dad. And when I tried to use the bathroom downstairs, the door was locked. I really, really, didn't mean to walk in on you."

I descended the stairs and made my way into the kitchen. I wanted to respond but I wasn't sure how. Either he did see something and now felt horrible for it, or he just felt horrible that he had to see me like that. Neither of those situations made me feel good at all.

So I turned, halting him inches from me. Whoa. Maybe I should have put on my brake lights first. "Listen, I get it Lucas. You didn't see anything. It was a mistake. Now, can we just forget it ever happened and move on?" I held his gaze and hopefully my ground, which felt as if it were crumbling.

I'd never seen him so...confused. It was almost shocking. He was the strong, confident one. Since when was he rattled?

I sighed as I turned back around and made my way to the

fridge where I pulled it open and studied the contents inside. I really didn't know what I wanted to eat, I just knew I couldn't stand there anymore, staring at the boy I was supposed to have platonic feelings for.

When I finally decided on frozen mozzarella sticks from the freezer, I shut the door and headed over to the oven. When Lucas didn't move to leave, I peeked over at him. "Hungry?" I asked and then winced. What was I doing? I couldn't get over Lucas when I was hanging out with him.

"Are you sure that's what you want?"

I slid my finger into the cardboard flap but paused as his words sunk around me. What did that mean? "Um, sure?" Was that what I was supposed to say?

He folded his arms and leaned against the counter as his eyebrows rose. "I'm just surprised. I mean, since you can't stand me and all."

My gaze whipped over to him and my heart sunk. He looked... hurt. He'd heard me and that bothered him. What was I supposed to think of that?

"I, um..." I let out my breath as I glanced around. What was I doing? This was the moment when I should tell him that he was right. I didn't like him. I needed to stop this. My relationship with my best friend was riding on this. But when I parted my lips, I couldn't make the words leave my mouth. "I didn't mean it like that."

Great. That's how you detract someone. Engage them.

He studied me. "What did you mean then?"

I pinched my lips together and turned, grateful for the distraction trying to find a cookie sheet for the mozzarella sticks brought me. Once I dumped them onto the sheet, I set them on top of the oven, taking my time and hoping to appear too busy to answer his question.

After I dusted off my hands, I turned, running right into Lucas' chest. I yelped as his hands surrounded my upper arms. I was pinned against him. I couldn't go anywhere. I was going to have to look up at him. Engage with him.

"Charlotte," he said. His warm tone washed over me, making me shiver.

Despite the warning bells going off in my mind, I glanced up. In that one moment, all of my resolve to leave Lucas to Maddie dissolved around me. All I could see was him. His brown eyes peering into my soul.

He didn't look angry or hurt anymore, just there. More present than anyone in my life had been in a long time. And he was searching my gaze. In that one look, I could see just what he wanted to know.

How I felt.

Pain, joy, fear, all of it coursed through me, causing my heart to pound and my head to swim. I couldn't do this. I couldn't. I wasn't ready. He didn't want to be with me.

Every doubt rushed through my mind, begging my feet to take a step back. Break the contact we had. Protect myself.

"If you didn't mean that, why did you say it?" His voice had grown husky as he leaned closer to me.

I blinked. I needed to speak. I needed to say something.

"You don't want to get involved with me," I said.

Wait, what? Why was I answering his question with that ridiculous comment? That's not what he asked. He wanted to know why I'd said something. Man, I was an idiot.

His expression softened as he searched my gaze. "What?"

I swallowed, heat settling in my cheeks. Well, I'd said it. I might as well own it. "You don't want anything to do with me. I'm...complicated."

A very irritating smile began to emerge on his lips. It wasn't mocking like the one I'd seen the first time I'd met him. It was more like he found me enduring. Like I was this little girl confessing her feelings for him.

I groaned as I stepped back. "This was a mistake—"

He grabbed my elbow and pulled me back. I crashed into his chest as his arms wrapped around me. My senses went haywire as I stood there, enveloped by his scent and the feeling of his skin against mine.

"What if I like complicated?" he asked, dipping down to meet my gaze. That movement brought his lips inches from mine.

Which he seemed to realize because his gaze flicked down to the lower half of my face before coming back up. I blinked as I forced those thoughts from my mind. We were just hugging. That didn't mean he liked me. Right?

"But you like Maddie," I said. Good. Bring up my best friend. Maybe that would help get his head on straight.

His brow furrowed. "I don't like Maddie."

Relief and worry conflicted inside of me. "What? Yes you do. You flirt with her all the time."

He studied me. "How could I be interested in Maddie when you're in the room?" He shook his head like that was the most ridiculous thought ever. "Maddie. She's a flirt, I'll admit. But she's not..." His voice trailed off as he focused his gaze back on me. "She's not you."

My heart took flight inside of my chest. It was the first time in my life that I was grateful for my ribcage and skin. Because at this moment, I was pretty sure my heart would have escaped, owned solely by Lucas.

I wanted to speak. Tell him he was a fool for picking me over Maddie. I wanted to list my faults. Tell him I wasn't worth his time. He could do so much better than me.

But when he raised his hand up to cup my cheek and ran his thumb over my lips, every thought I had left. Poof. Gone.

"Charlotte, you are someone special. I can't stop thinking about you since the moment I stupidly spilled my coffee on you."

Ooo, score one for Charlotte. Lucas finally admitted that *he* spilled his coffee on me. And that it might have been wrong

He chuckled and said, "Yes. I was a jerk."

Hmm, maybe I'm not as mysterious as I thought I was. He could obviously read me like a book.

"If getting stuck in Sweet Water means meeting you, then I'd do it over and over again." He lowered his hand and wrapped his arm around my back, pulling me so close that it took my breath away.

My ears were ringing and I wondered if he'd really said what I thought he did, or was I just imagining it. "Really?" I asked as I held his gaze.

He studied me for a moment longer before he leaned closer. "Really." With that last word, he pressed his lips to mine.

Warmth spread across my body as I reveled in the feeling of him against me. I pushed out all doubts that this wasn't really happening as I ran my hands from his shoulders, up to his neck, and then twisted my fingers into his hair.

His kiss was soft at first, as if he were asking me for permission. Deciding to throw caution to the wind, I pressed my body as close to him as possible as I rose up onto my tiptoes. Anything I could do to invite him to continue.

He must have picked up on my hint because suddenly, I was airborne. He'd pulled me up, and out of instinct I wrapped my legs around his waist. Holding onto me with one hand, he used his other to feel for the countertop where he set me down.

"Charlotte," he murmured through our joined lips.

Tingles erupted throughout my body as I parted my lips, and deepened the kiss.

I'm not sure how long we kissed, but it felt like an eternity. A long, blissful, I-don't-want-this-to-stop, eternity.

When I was wrapped up in Lucas's arms, I wasn't the girl who lost her mom to cancer. And I wasn't the girl whose dad collected everything imaginable just to keep his mind off said mom.

I was Charlotte. Being with him meant I could be myself and that was okay. I didn't have to be strong because he was there, holding me up.

He pulled back to study me and I groaned. My lips feel puffy and my eyelids heavy as I met his gaze. This time, I held it. I wanted him to see everything. I wanted him to know how I felt.

He narrowed his eyes. "I like you, Charlotte."

I chewed my lip and couldn't help the smile that spread across my face. It was like my birthday and Christmas all wrapped up into one glorious moment.

I finally felt happy and it had been a long time since I'd felt that emotion. I grabbed onto his shoulders and pulled him toward me, pressing my lips to his.

He chuckled as he pulled back, staying inches from my face. "This is normally where you say something."

I faked a confused look and then giggled when he poked me in the ribs. Then, I steadied my gaze as I held it. "I like you, too, Lucas Addington."

He grinned, sending my heart soaring as he leaned forward and kissed both of my cheeks, the tip of my nose, and then my forehead.

Frustrated with his teasing, I moved my face so the logical next option was my lips. He obliged and we fell into a rhythm and it felt so complete. Like there was nothing else in the world I was meant to do but kiss Lucas.

And for now, I was going to think that. Because despite my best efforts to ignore the sinking feeling in my stomach, I knew, at some point, I was going to have to tell Maddie and that thought scared me more than anything right now.

So, I was going to push it to the farthest regions of my mind and bask in the happiness I felt by being with Lucas. I needed this. For now.

CHAPTER SIXTEEN

"I can't believe it!" Quinn's voice rose so high that I could hear it as I pulled the receiver from my face. I couldn't help the grin that spread across my face from her excitement.

It had been exactly two hours since Lucas and I had declared our feelings for each other and we were currently cuddling on the couch, watching a chick flick...and kissing. That was, until Quinn called.

Now, we were both grinning at each other as we told his sister that we were somewhat dating. I still wasn't sure what we were, we really hadn't put a label on anything yet.

"I'm so mad I'm not there with you guys." Her voice drifted off and for a moment, she wasn't that carefree girl I'd met a week ago. Something was up. I glanced over at Lucas who seemed to have picked up on her tone as well.

"What did Dad do?" he asked.

I studied him. His cold demeanor had emerged and suddenly, I realized, his dad had banished him here, and I still didn't know why. He must have felt me staring because suddenly, his gaze met mine. He held it as he listened to Quinn.

"Yeah. Well, you know our parents. Everyone is wrong for us if they aren't the ones they picked for us."

My brow furrowed as I flicked my gaze to the phone. What did that mean, picked for them? When I returned my gaze to Lucas, I saw him studying me. I gave him a smile, just to let him know that all was good even if I couldn't quite figure out what Quinn was saying.

"Hey sis, I gotta go. Call you later?"

"Yeah, sure. Make sure to call me though, I need to talk to you about something. Charlotte?"

I turned my attention to the phone. "Yeah?"

"Remember, I still want you in New York. Find a way to come visit me. I miss your face."

I nodded, the feeling of happiness swelling up inside of my chest. I really liked Quinn. A lot. "Of course. I'm excited for it."

Quinn said her goodbyes and Lucas hung up the phone. He set it down next to him and then tightened his arm that was around my shoulder and pulled me close. We sat there for a few minutes until I pulled back to study him.

He kept his gaze frozen on the TV in front of us. I could tell he was purposely ignoring me. I waited until he finally looked over at me.

"What?" he asked.

I studied him. Was he serious? "So are your parents old school or something?"

Lucas sighed as he pushed his free hand through his hair. "My parents are snobs. That's all you need to know."

I quirked an eyebrow, hoping that told him there was no way I was going to accept that answer.

He growled as he shifted to sit up higher. "My parents feel that being wealthy is a gene or something. And they only want their children to date other rich kids. It's sick how much they try to control us."

I was listening to him but I really wasn't. All I could focus on were two little words. Wealthy and mingle. Did that mean his parents would frown on our...whatever this was?

Suddenly, he turned, grabbing both my shoulders with his hands and turning me to face him. "Listen to me, it's ridiculous. And I won't stand for it."

I met his gaze, but my body felt light. Like this wasn't really happening. I'd finally let myself care for someone only to find out that I just might be the Juliet to his Romeo. Were his parents ever going to accept me? "Is that why they sent you to Sweet Water? Because of a girl?"

He studied me for a moment before he let go of me and flopped back on the couch, letting his breath out in an exaggerated movement. When he didn't respond, my whole body went numb. It was true. He'd fallen for another girl and was sent to Sweet Water as punishment. Did that mean when his parents found out about me, he'd be sent away?

"Her name was Maggie. She was a girl I'd met through a friend. I, um..." He paused, looking over at me.

I gave him a weak smile, but inside, I was dying. There was no way I wanted to hear about his previous girlfriends, but I needed to know the truth.

"I was stupid. I believed she liked me. I let her convince me to do some stupid things." He scrubbed his face and then tipped his head back so he was studying the ceiling. "The biggest thing was probably letting her convince me to take out my family's yacht. While we were on it, Maggie asked if she could steer. I was drunk and stupid so I let her."

He closed his eyes and I could see the stress and regret etched on his features. "I don't know how it happened, but she crashed the yacht into some rocks and when I finally found her, she was in the water. I thought she was drowning so I went in to get her."

His voice trailed off, and he grew quiet. I stared at him, not sure if I should answer him or not. I went with not and instead, leaned against the back of the couch and brought my knees up to my chest to hug them.

When he finally glanced over at me, my breath hitched in my throat. He was hurting. Bad. I reached out and ran my fingers through his hair. Anything to let him know that I was here.

He closed his eyes and leaned into my palm. "I was stupid," he said. His voice was low and filled with regret.

I shook my head. He must have felt the movement because his eyes opened and his gaze landed on me.

"Yeah, I am. I thought she was hurt. I let myself care." He straightened. "She just wanted my family's money. She sued us."

My eyes widened as my jaw dropped. That was not what I was expecting him to say. "She what?"

His gaze dipped down to his hands which he clasped in his lap. "She sued us. My dad settled it out of court. He didn't want the stain on the Addington name." His voice grew softer. "Then he shipped his mistake of a son away to think about what he'd done."

I reached out and grasped his hands with my own. There was no way I was going to sit there and let him believe that he was a mistake. "It wasn't your fault."

Lucas hesitated and then shrugged, effectively pulling his hands from mine. "It doesn't matter. It's over. I don't care how much my dad wants me to rethink what happened so that I can finally reclaim my place in the Addington fortune. I'm going to choose who I care about." He watched me for a moment, before turning to face me head on. "And that person is you."

I smiled, ignoring the sinking feeling that was settling in my gut. Lucas seemed confident that we could make it work and knew better than me, right?

He leaned forward and pressed his lips to mine. I sunk into the kiss as I snuggled closer to him. There was a hint of desperation in his movements, like he needed the reassurance as well.

I decided to stop thinking about everything. If I did, I feared what I might do. If I cared about Lucas and Lucas cared about me, it shouldn't matter what everyone else thought. Right?

The sound of the back-door slamming pulled us apart. I glanced toward the kitchen to see Dad studying us, his eyebrows raised.

Lucas was off the couch and rubbing his palms on his pants as he straightened and turned to Dad. "Hey, Mr. Robinson," he said.

I shot Dad a panicked look, which I prayed he picked up on. Dad studied me for a moment with a quirked eyebrow before turning his attention back to Lucas. "Get that work done?" he asked, dumping the plastic bags in his hands onto the counter behind him.

"Um, yes. Well, sort of. I got part of it done." Lucas glanced over at me and then back to Dad. "I'll go out and finish up." He nodded at me before he hurried out of the house, shutting the outside door behind him.

I watched his hasty retreat and once he was gone, I turned to glare at Dad. "Did you have to freak him out like that? And where's Drew?" I glanced out the window only to see Drew sprinting around in the backyard. He then zeroed in on Lucas and rushed over to him. My heart swelled when Lucas reached out and tousled his hair and then motioned for Drew to follow him.

Dad's movement drew my attention over to him as he took out a container of yogurt and cheese from the bag and then made his way over to the fridge. "So, something changed while we were gone?" Dad's voice was low and hard to read. Was he mad?

"Yeah, well…" I wasn't really sure how I was supposed to end that sentence. If it were Mom, it would be a no brainer. But Dad? Ugh.

When he turned around, his eyebrows were raised as if he were waiting for me to answer. When I didn't, he asked, "So are you and Lucas an item?"

I scrunched up my nose. "No one says that anymore."

Dad held up his hands. "Okay. If you're not that, then what's happening? I mean, from what I've seen, you two aren't just friends."

I groaned as I grabbed out the box of granola bars that he had in the bag and opened it up. Just now, I realized I'd completely forgotten to put the mozzarella sticks into the oven and I was starving. Man, I was a basket case.

I peeled off the wrapper and threw it into the garbage, trying to buy time before I had to answer.

Dad sighed as he turned back to the bags. "I know your mom was better at this 'being a girl' stuff, but I want you to know that I'm here."

I almost choked on the granola bar. It'd been so long since I had heard Dad talk about Mom—it was shocking to hear her name come from his lips. And the fact that he was trying to be a dad was strange as well. All I could do was nod, even though I was pretty sure he could read the shocked expression on my face.

He studied me for a moment more and then nodded. "Great. Well, no more staying in the house alone together if you two are making this into something more."

I nodded again, heat rushing to my cheeks. It felt good for someone else to acknowledge that Lucas and I were something. Right now, there were very few people I could actually tell about Lucas and I. It felt good to admit it, even if it was my dad. Hearing it said out loud made what happened between Lucas and I more real.

Like my life as this lonely blob floating through space just might be coming to an end. With Lucas by my side, there wasn't much I couldn't do.

Dad seemed to have moved on. He finished unloading the groceries and was holding up the cookie sheet of mozzarella sticks. "You finished with these?"

I nodded as exhaustion took over and I made my way to the stairs. "Yeah, I forgot about those."

Dad moved over to the garbage where he dumped the half-thawed sticks into the garbage.

"I'm heading to bed. Last day of summer tomorrow."

Dad nodded and waved me away as he turned to the sink to start the dishes.

I took the stairs two at a time. Once I was in my room, I raced to the window where I saw Lucas standing by the Chevy. He was studying the engine as if he were trying to figure something out.

Drew was pushing his scooter around in circles and I could tell from his lips, he was chatting away at Lucas.

My heart picked up speed as I watched them. It felt so right to see him standing in my yard, talking to my baby brother.

I tapped on my window, hoping he'd hear. It took a few times before his gaze made its way up to me. When it met mine, my toes tingled as I opened my hand into a wave.

He gave me a wink and then pressed his lips to his fingers and blew me a kiss. I pretended to catch it and then pressed my hand to my heart.

He lifted his thumb and pinkie to his face to indicate that I call him. Heat rushed over my skin as I nodded. After one final look—when his features stilled and the intensity from his gaze almost melted the glass in front of me—I blew him a kiss and backed away from the window.

There was no way I was going to be able to sleep with the emotions rushing through my body so I just flopped down on my bed and pulled my phone from my pocket. My stomach sank when I realized that I'd missed a call from Maddie.

I laid my phone on my chest and closed my eyes. What was wrong with me? Regret and worry flooded my body as I swallowed. A wave of sadness washed over me when my first thought was to talk to Mom, only to remember that she was gone and I was alone.

I loved Dad, but there was no way he could advise me on something like this.

My phone chimed again and I raised it to see another message from Maddie had come in.

Maddie: *Wanna get pizza tomorrow? I need a reason to see Lucas. I feel like the bait is set, I just need to reel him in.*

Ugh. I was in so much trouble.

I swear I started and deleted about thirty responses to her until I settled on:

Me: *Sure. What time?*

I held my breath as I waited for an answer.

Maddie: *Noon. My house. We'll get pizza and then you and I can go to the mall for some final school shopping.*

I sent her a smiley emoji and a thumbs-up emoji, and then set my phone on the nightstand. Well, I had about fifteen hours to figure out how exactly I was going to tell Maddie about Lucas without ruining our friendship.

I covered my face with my arm and groaned.

I was in trouble.

CHAPTER SEVENTEEN

*T*he next morning, I woke up with a knot in my stomach. I flipped from one side of the bed to the other, but nothing helped alleviate the feeling of guilt that had lodged itself in every crevice of my body.

I flipped to my back and studied the ceiling.

"I like Lucas and Lucas likes me," I said to the air.

It was so simple, just seven little words. They couldn't be that bad, right?

Wrong.

It was going to devastate Maddie. She was not going to take this well.

Maybe I could figure out a way to not tell her. That would be so much easier. I could just pretend that he didn't exist.

I let out a sigh. That wasn't fair to him or Maddie. I needed to be honest even if it meant I might lose my best friend.

Just thinking the words made me want to throw up. Pushing them from my mind, I pulled my covers from my body and stood. I needed a hot shower, then I'd feel better.

It took twenty minutes of me standing in the hot water to realize, nothing was going to make me feel better. So I flipped off the shower and stepped out.

Once my hair was dry and pulled back into a ponytail, I put on a little bit of makeup and dressed in a pair of shorts and a flowy peasant top. I didn't look like I was trying too hard, but I also didn't look like the frumpy girl that so many people were used to.

I descended the stairs to find Dad in the kitchen, whipping up some pancakes. My mouth watered as I stared at the man who, for the longest time, had given up on life. All he'd cared about since Mom's death was buying beat up cars. Cooking us breakfast was not on the top of his list.

"Good morning, sweetie," he said, stopping to lean over and kiss my cheek.

"Okay, who are you and what did you do with my dad?"

He feigned a shocked expression as he turned back to the griddle and flipped a few pancakes.

"Daddy made Star War shaped pancakes," Drew exclaimed through a mouthful of pancakes and syrup. He waved to his half eaten Yoda.

I raised my eyebrows at Dad. "Wow. That's…creative."

Dad raised his spatula. "I can make you a Princess Leia."

I shook my head and grabbed a few pancakes from the top of the stack. "I'm good. I'll be fine with these."

Dad just shrugged. "Suit yourself."

After slathering them with syrup, I grabbed a fork and settled down at the table.

My phone chimed just as I slipped the first bite into my mouth. My heart soared when I saw it was a text from Lucas.

Lucas: *Hey beautiful. Can I see you after work?*

I swallowed as nerves rose up in my stomach. I wanted to see him so bad, but I couldn't focus on that right now. I needed to have my wits about me when I saw Maddie this afternoon.

But I also couldn't just leave him hanging.

Me: *I'll see if I have room in my schedule.*

Lucas texted a shocked faced emoji.

I giggled as I responded with a shrug. Just as I hit send, I got another text, this time, from Winny.

Winny: *SOS I need you to come in this morning. Think you have the time?*

I studied her words. Winny was not a panicking sort of person. It worried me that she would act this way. I glanced up to Dad. "Can I go to Winny's this morning?" A feeling of worry compounded the feeling of excitement at the thought of seeing Lucas, so much so that my appetite dissolved.

Dad glanced up. "I, um...well..." I stared at him. Why was he acting so cryptic? Before I asked, he nodded. "Yeah. I guess that's fine. I will need you to watch Drew this evening. I have...a meeting to go to."

I studied him. "Meeting?" I did not like the sound of that.

Dad just shrugged. "Adult stuff. You'll be fine."

Before I could respond, my phone chimed again. This time it was Maddie confirming out shopping plans. I sent her a thumbs up and then turned back to Dad only to have him turn on the radio and blast the music as he started filling up the sink with water and soap.

Drew started singing along with Dad and I realized there was no way I was going to get a straight answer from him. Not right now.

So I stood and set my plate down on the counter next to the sink and shot Dad a pointed look. He just shrugged and reached up to dollop some soap bubbles on my nose.

Frustrated, I wiped them off and then made my way to the door where I slipped on my shoes. I hated that he was keeping something from me. It was like I was back to when Mom was sick and they were keeping that a secret from us. I deserved to know what was going on.

I blew out my breath realizing that perhaps, I was just frustrated with everything in my life and not just Dad's cryptic meeting. I just needed to relax before I freaked out over nothing.

I climbed onto my bike and started down the streets of Sweet Water. I let my worries and thoughts flow away with the wind. Excitement built up inside of me as I pulled behind the Bread Basket and pushed the kickstand down.

I jogged up the back steps and pulled open the back door only to be met with Lucas' grinning face. I yelped as I jumped back, startled by his sudden appearance.

But before I could react, he had his hands around my waist and was pulling me toward him, pressing his lips against mine. I giggled as I wrapped my arms around his neck and pressed in closer to him. Here is where I belonged. There was nowhere else I'd rather be than snuggled next to Lucas. He made me feel safe and cared about. Nothing mattered when he was around.

I groaned when he pulled back and rested his forehead against mine.

"Hey," he said. His voice was low and deep and sent shivers down my back.

"Hey," I said. I sounded just as breathy as I felt.

"I'm glad you're here."

Suddenly remembering Winny's panicked text, I pulled away to glance toward the kitchen. "Is she okay? She seemed pretty worried when she texted me."

Lucas followed my gaze with his own and then turned to look at me. "I don't know. She's been pretty quiet today. Mostly cleaning."

I stared at him as I processed his words. What did that mean? "Cleaning? Winny's the most sanitary person I know."

Lucas shrugged as he reached down and grabbed my hand, threading his fingers through mine. "She won't talk to me," he said as he brought our grasped hands up to press his lips against my fingers.

Huh. That's weird. I turned to him and gave him a sheepish

look. "I love all of this"—his eyebrows rose right when I said the word love—"I mean, like, all of this, but I should go see what she needs."

Lucas groaned but nodded. "Yeah. It seems like she needs a friend."

I gave him a thankful smile, rose up onto my toes to press my lips to his, and then stepped away from him. He held onto my fingers as long as he could before distance broke us apart. My body felt cold in his absence but I didn't let that dissuade me. Winny needed my help and I was here to offer it.

Lucas had been truthful. I found Winny elbow deep in scrubbing out the pantry. She'd moved all the contents from the shelves and was wiping down the wood and containers.

"Hey, Winny," I said as I stepped up to her.

She whipped around at the sound of my voice. "Char!" She exclaimed, reaching over to pull me into a hug. I patted her back as she squeezed me. "I'm so happy you are here."

She pulled back. I had to admit, something was up. She had this crazed look in her eye.

"Everything okay?" I asked.

She nodded but that slowly morphed into her shaking her head. "No. Not really. I just found out my son wants to visit."

I stared at her as her sentence slowly sank in. Her son? Did she mean Lucas' dad?

"He—your what?" I asked, hoping maybe I misheard.

Winny pulled off her yellow gloves to rub her temples. "I got his message today. He wants to see how Lucas is doing and check out the shop." She took in a shaky breath. "I've never been this nervous in my life."

I glanced toward the back where I had last seen Lucas. I wondered if he was still there, listening to this conversation. "Does Lucas know?" I asked, leaning into her. I wasn't sure what his dad's sudden appearance would do to our relationship.

Winny shook her head. "No. I haven't told him. With how

things are between them, I don't want to. I'm hoping it's just a one stop visit and he'll be on his way."

I nodded. I knew I should feel bad about keeping this a secret from Lucas but I agreed with Winny. With how he felt about his dad, I didn't want him to suddenly shut down. We were finally moving forward with our relationship and I didn't want that to mar it. Thankfully, Winny dropped the subject and we just focused on cleaning.

I was in the shop wiping down the shelves and baskets when Lucas strode into the room with his pizza hat and shirt on. He looked...adorable. And normal. And not like he came from a family worth billions.

I swallowed when I saw him, the news of his dad's sudden appearance on the tip of my tongue. Maybe if I just didn't speak to him, I might actually be able to keep that secret.

"Going out?" I asked, glancing down at my watch and realizing I had an hour until I needed to meet up with Maddie.

He didn't stop until his arms were wrapped around my waist and he was pulling me close. "Yeah. Gotta make that money." He dipped down and brushed his lips to mine.

Call me crazy, but keeping a secret from Lucas made me feel horrible. So much so that I didn't feel right kissing him. Or letting him think that I was the upfront and honest person—when I wasn't.

He must have sensed my hesitation because he pulled away and studied me. "What's wrong?"

I pressed my lips together and stepped over toward the basket I'd been cleaning. "Nothing. I'm just trying to help Winny out."

He nodded, glancing around. Thankfully he didn't seem tipped off at all. Instead, he was calm. "Did you figure out why she suddenly wanted to do some spring cleaning?"

I wasn't sure what to do so I just shrugged. "She gets like this sometimes. It's best to just help and stay out of her way."

He chuckled as he grabbed Winny's keys from his front pocket.

"Well, I should get going. Can't wait until I have my own wheels." He winked at me.

Heat rushed to my cheeks as I couldn't help but smile back at him. "Oh yeah?"

He nodded and then leaned forward to press his lips to my cheek. "But I will enjoy my time at your house until then." He pulled back and focused his gaze, the intensity making me melt where I stood.

"I agree," I whispered.

He winked and then pulled back. "See ya, Winny," he said.

I jumped and turned to see Winny standing in the doorway to the kitchen. She had a rag and spray bottle in her hand and a shocked look on her face.

"Bye," she managed before turning to stare at me.

Too embarrassed to speak, I returned to my rag and basket, hoping she'd just let this go. But, when I saw her approach from the side, I knew that hope was a futile one.

"So, you and Lucas?" she asked.

I pinched my lips together as worry rushed through my body, making it feel hot. "Yep. Mm hmm," I muttered when it seemed like she wanted a response.

When she didn't answer, I glanced up. Her expression shocked me. She didn't look angry or happy. Just sad.

Which confused me. "Is that okay?" I managed to ask. Fear was gripping my throat and I wasn't sure I wanted to hear her response but I needed to know.

Winny focused on me and a look of realization flashed over her face. "Oh, sweetie, I didn't mean it like that. It's just that...well, my son is picky. He's not going to be happy with Lucas dating anyone without a trust fund."

I blew out my breath as I fought the tears that formed. It was bad enough to hear it from Lucas and yet, it was ten times harder to hear it from Winny. I focused on a stain in front of me, rubbing it as hard as I could even though I knew it was never going to come off.

Suddenly, Winny's hand appeared in my line of sight, halting my scrubbing.

"It's not about you, sweetie. It's wrong how Keith views the world. He gets it...from his dad."

I could feel the tears brimming on my lids as I brought my gaze up. "Keith?"

"My son. Lucas' dad."

I swallowed and nodded. For some reason, even the simplest words were confusing me.

"I met Keith's dad when he was poor. He always loved money and lord, that man worked. All the time. I got sick of it and left once I found out that he'd cheated on me. I wanted Keith but his dad won the custody battle. I saw Keith occasionally, but when he saw how I lived compared to his dad, he wanted nothing to do with me."

She paused, staring off in the distance as her words sunk around us. I wasn't sure if I should start speaking or wait.

I parted my lips, but she continued.

"Now, he's picky. Feels like people who don't have money aren't worth his time. I guess he sent Lucas here to punish him. What he didn't realize was that it would break my heart." She swallowed as her voice broke. My heart went out to her and all I wanted to do was give her a hug. "Who wants to be told that their house is the timeout spot? Like no one would want to come here unless they wanted to be miserable."

Frustrated and angry with Lucas' dad, I reached over and pulled Winny into a hug. There was no way I was going to let this guy into our lives if he was just going to hurt us like this. And I was pretty sure, Lucas wouldn't let that happen.

"He's a fool," I muttered into her shoulder as I squeezed her.

Her arms surrounded me. "Thanks, Char. You are such a sweetie. I'm blessed to have you in my life."

Tears were flowing now as I pulled back and nodded. "Me too."

Winny reached up and wiped my tears from cheeks. "You shouldn't cry. You are such a strong girl. I'm honored to work alongside you."

I nodded. Truth was. I felt the same. We stood in silence for a few moments before Winny took a deep breath and glanced around.

"Well, we already started this spring cleaning. Might as well finish it," she said, giving me a wink.

I glanced at my watch. I had exactly forty-five minutes until I needed to leave. I could help her until then. I owed it to her.

CHAPTER EIGHTEEN

I climbed up the front steps of Maddie's house exactly at noon. I tried to feel happy but I swear, if there had been background music, it would have been the funeral march. I had no idea how Maddie would react to anything I told her, and if I was honest, I wasn't sure how I felt about anything after my conversation with Winny.

I knew Lucas came from a complicated family, I just didn't realize how complicated.

I took a deep breath as I reached out and pressed on her doorbell. It dinged inside and a few seconds later, Maddie appeared. She was wearing a short, black miniskirt and a floral tank.

"Char," she exclaimed as she stepped out onto the porch to hug me.

Ugh. Regret. Betrayal. All the things I was going to feel now that I was knowingly deceiving my best friend. I was the worst.

"Hey, Mads," I said as she led the way into her house and shut the door behind me.

Cool air surrounded me as I slipped off my shoes. I could hear her twin brothers wrestling in the toy room in the back of the house. "Watching Easton and Weston?" I asked, nodding in the direction of the noise.

She rolled her eyes. "Yeah. Until mom gets back. Which she promised would be in an hour." Then she clasped her hands together. "Just enough time for Lucas to deliver the pizza," she said, wiggling her eyebrows.

Not sure what to do, I just nodded. How long could I keep this up? I mean, she was falling for Lucas and here I was, letting her even though I knew he wasn't interested. Pushing aside the ache in my gut, I turned and made my way into her kitchen, suddenly feeling very thirsty.

"Ready for tomorrow?" I asked as I pressed the glass to the button on the fridge. Ice-cold water poured out.

Maddie sighed as she slipped onto the bar stool and leaned on the island in the middle of the kitchen. "To do the school work? No. But I'm excited that it's our senior year. And if I show up with the hot new guy, I think it will be a good omen for the rest of the year."

Cool water flowed over my fingers, shocking me. I glanced down to see that I'd let the water overflow. I cursed myself under my breath as I pulled the glass away from the button and set it down on the counter in front of me.

Maddie appeared with a dishrag and helped me mop up the excess water. I thanked her and then straightened. I was a terrible person and yet here she was, helping me out.

After I downed the water, I leaned against the counter and glanced over at her. She was studying me, her brow furrowed.

"You okay?" she asked. I could hear a hint of concern in her voice.

Great. This was not going well. Not sure what to do, I just nodded. "Yeah, uh huh. I'm just...nervous. Dad said something cryptic about a meeting tonight and I'm worried."

Relief flooded my body. Finally, I had something else to talk about instead of Lucas. And then the realization that the something else was my dad being cryptic, which was never a good sign.

Maddie was nodding and I could see the wheels turning in her mind. "What do you think it is?" Then she leaned forward. "Do you think he's dating?"

I scrunched up my nose. "No, but now I am."

Maddie shrugged. "He's cute, you know, for a dad. I can see him dating."

I held up my hands. There was no way I wanted her to continue this train of thought. "I think that's enough," I said. And then I let every possibility, besides my dad dating, enter my mind. The largest one, in big, neon letters, was *Scrap Yard*. It played over and over like a skipping CD.

"Do you think it has to do with our yard?" Worry crept up in my chest and I swallowed, hoping to push it down.

Maddie chewed her nail. "Well, I didn't before but now that you mention it, that could be it. I mean, the last time I saw Mrs. Protresca, she did not look happy."

My stomach sank at Maddie's words. It had to be our yard. I mean, what else could it be?

The doorbell rang, breaking up our conversation. Maddie squealed and sprinted toward the door and it wasn't until I heard Lucas' voice, that I realized what this meant.

Lucas was here, in Maddie's clutches. There was no way she was going to let him go free. And I hadn't confessed what had happened the night before. This was going to be pure torture.

"Come on back," Maddie called in a singsong voice.

I wanted to sprint from the room. To hide and never come back. Right now, I was lying to the people who meant the most to me. Lucas about his dad and Maddie about Lucas. I was the worst.

Lucas was carrying a box in front of him and his eyebrows went up when he saw me. "Charlotte," he said as he set the pizza down in front of him.

"Lucas," I said, nodding in his direction.

He studied me and I couldn't really tell what he was thinking. Instead, I forced a relaxed smile, which he must have taken differently because he motioned to Maddie and asked, "You told her?"

Just as the words left his lips, my whole body went numb. I whipped my gaze over to Maddie, who was staring at Lucas and then moved her gaze to me.

"Tell me what?"

Lucas' cheeks went red as I saw him swallow. Hard. "I—er... the pizza's on the house," he said as he turned and made his way to the front door. I could see him as he twisted the handle and then turned to meet my gaze.

I could see the pain and worry in it as he mouthed *I'm sorry.*

All I could do was shrug. Well, the cat was out of the bag. I might as well tell Maddie. Besides, she was staring me down and making me feel as if I was going to melt on the spot.

"What do you need to tell me?" she asked. Well, not really asked, but more dictated.

I wanted to hide right there. I hated the fact that I was about to betray my best friend.

"Lucas and I like each other," tumbled from my lips.

Maddie parted her lips as she stared at me. I could see the questions and anger forming on her face. "What?"

"I didn't know, I swear. I just...we just..." I sighed, the pain of holding on to so many things came crashing down around me. Why couldn't I ever make the right choice? Instead of muttering nonsensical things, I just pinched my lips shut and shrugged.

"How long have you liked him?" Her gaze and tone had turned icy. She was not happy.

Knowing I couldn't keep lying to my friend, I shrugged. "I don't know, Maddie. It's been complicated between Lucas and I." I slumped against the counter and sighed.

The sound of the pizza box opening drew my attention over. Maddie had pulled out a slice and was breaking off bits and slipping them into her mouth.

"You lied to me. You let me believe that you didn't like him. You told me to my face that you didn't like him. You didn't stop me from pursuing him." Her eyes had narrowed as she continued eating at a frantic pace.

A storm cloud of frustration and anger settled inside of me. "Yeah, well, you flirt with just about every guy. How was I supposed to know that you really liked Lucas? That he wasn't just a guy for you to conquer?"

As soon as the words left my lips, I regretted them. I wanted to suck them back into my mouth and forget about this stupid argument. Since when was I the kind of person that let a relationship, or a guy, come between me and a best friend? I wasn't *that* girl.

Maddie's expression froze for a moment before she pushed away from the counter and waved toward the door. "I think you should go."

I parted my lips as I stared at her. Was she serious? I mean, we could get through this, couldn't we? Our years of friendship had to withstand this. It had to.

"Maddie, come on," I said. I wasn't opposed to begging. I'd do it if it meant we could put this behind us.

Maddie just shook her head as she waved her hand toward the door. "I'm just not in the mood to hang out anymore. Besides, I've got to watch my brothers and feed them. I'd rather do that alone."

My ears were ringing as I grabbed my purse and pushed the strap up onto my shoulder. I started to speak, but from the look on Maddie's face, she didn't want to hear it so I pinched my lips shut.

She was just upset with me. It didn't mean that we were done as friends. We could get through this, I was certain of it...well, maybe certain was a strong word. I *hoped* we'd get through this.

I made my way to her front door and reached out to grab the handle. I turned it but then stopped. I couldn't leave without at least apologizing. I owed it to her. After everything we'd been through together, I couldn't leave her thinking I hated her.

"I'm sorry, Mads," I said, offering her an apologetic smile.

She had her arms folded over her chest and she was staring out the window to the left of where we stood. I could tell she was hurt. Her face was contorted into a look of pain as she took in a deep breath.

"I just can't talk to you right now," she whispered.

The hollow feeling in the pit of my stomach deepened as I swallowed and nodded. I knew that I had been a terrible friend. I deserved her cold demeanor.

"Okay," I said as I pulled open her front door and walked out onto the porch. I didn't look back as I shut the door and headed down the steps and over to my bike. Tears blurred my vision as I climbed onto my seat and set my feet on the pedals.

It was a good thing I knew exactly where I was going because I could only partially see the road and street signs. But I'd biked to Maddie's more times then I could count. I knew the path like the back of my hand.

Ten minutes later, I pulled into our yard and dropped the bike down on the grass. I didn't look around as I climbed our steps and moved to pull open the door. A piece of paper that was tacked to the door halted me in my steps.

I blinked a few times as I studied the words written on it.

Seizure of Property

My already aching stomach plummeted to the ground. I rubbed my eyes as I skimmed the paper. We needed to clean up the yard of all the vehicles or the city would seize the property. We had one week to make progress.

I swallowed as I glanced around. Where was Dad? He had to have seen this. I'd been right all along. The meeting tonight had to be about our house.

I pushed open the front door and slammed it closed—probably harder than I needed to. I slipped off my shoes and pushed my hair from my face. Sweat had caused it to cling to my face.

"Dad?" I yelled, glancing around the stairs to the kitchen.

That's when I saw him. He was sitting at the table with his shoulders slumped. His head was down and I could tell the weight of the world was bearing down on him.

Frustration and sympathy coursed through my body causing me to shake. I didn't want to be angry with him. How could I? He was hurting, just like me.

I took in a deep breath and made my way over to him. Even though snippy comments were racing through my mind, I pushed them aside. That was the last thing he needed.

"Hey, Dad," I said, reaching out and resting my hand on his shoulder.

He glanced over at me and I almost took a step back. His eyes and nose were puffy. My gaze flicked down to his hands, which were holding a picture of Mom.

I stared at her familiar dark hair and equally dark eyes. I was a baby and she was holding me up to her face as she smiled at the camera. I couldn't tear my eyes away from the photo. It'd been so long since I'd seen her face, it was like I'd forgotten what she looked like.

But now that I was staring at it, all the memories I held came crashing into my mind. Tears slid down my cheeks as I pulled out a chair and sat down next to Dad.

We sat in silence until Dad let out his breath. "You saw the note?" he asked.

I nodded, reaching up to wipe the tears from my face. "Yeah. It's not fair. They can't do this."

Dad handed the photo over to me and I gingerly took it. He then leaned back in his chair and scrubbed his face with his hands. "They can and they will. I thought I might be able to convince them to extend the deadline." He reached out and pushed a stack of papers toward me.

I skimmed them and realized, this wasn't the first notice the city had sent. From the size of the stack, they'd been trying to get Dad to clean up the yard for a while now.

"Dad, what...?" I asked, as I lifted the corner of the papers and let them fall one at a time onto each other.

His shoulders slumped further. "I know. I know. I'm a mess. I just..." His voice broke and drifted off as he ran his hands through his hair.

It hurt so much to see him sitting there so broken. He was trying to be strong for us. I knew he was trying. But, just like me, he was failing. At least we were failing together.

I reached out and covered his hands with mind. "So, what do we do?" We couldn't just sit there, wallowing, we needed to be active.

Dad glanced up at me and I could see the pain in his gaze. "I don't know."

I nodded. It had to be a lot for someone who had refused to face the death of his wife and refused to adapt to his new life without her.

"We have to get rid of the cars, Dad." I studied him, waiting to see how he'd take that.

He got a far-off expression on his face before determination took over and he stood. "This is ridiculous. I mean, I pay taxes. I should be able to put whatever I want on my lawn."

He stormed over to the front door and pulled it open, stepping onto the porch. "You hear that Sweet Water? A Robinson can do whatever the hell he wants to with his property!" He then turned and pulled the sign off the door, crumpled it up, and threw it into the corner of the porch.

Anxiety crept up in my chest as I stood and rushed over to him. I gave him a look that I hoped told him I was not pleased with his behavior and then walked over to grab the crumpled paper.

"You can't do that, Dad," I said as I attempted to smooth the paper on the porch railing only to pull too hard which ripped it halfway.

Sweat beaded on my forehead as frustration and anger pricked my spine. I had never felt more alone than I did right now. How was everything around me disintegrating?

At least I still had Lucas.

I shot Dad another disapproving look, but he didn't seem to notice. Instead, he paced the porch, glaring at cars that drove by. Realizing that I wasn't going to change his mind—at least not right now—I stepped into the house and over to his desk where I pulled out the tape.

I'd fix this problem and then I'd go upstairs to brainstorm everything else that had gone south in my life.

After the note was tacked back onto the door, I commanded Dad not to touch it and then made my way back inside and up to my room. I collapsed on my bed and pulled out my phone.

Right now, I needed Lucas more than anything. I was about to break and he was the only thing keeping me together.

CHAPTER NINETEEN

I must have been exhausted because I fell asleep on my bed, waiting for Lucas to call me back. After 10 texts and 15 voicemails, I'd finally given up on him responding and distracted myself with ridiculous cat videos.

Two hours later, I woke up to my phone ringing and a drool stain on my comforter. Nice. If only Lucas was here to see how classy I was, I'm sure it would cement our relationship.

I pushed myself up to sitting as I glanced down at my phone.

Lucas.

My heart thrummed in my chest as I pressed the green button and brought the phone to my cheek.

"Hey," I said, my voice still breathy with sleep.

"Hey. You called?"

I hesitated, taking note of his icy tone. What was that about?

"Yeah. How was work?"

He paused before responding. "Good."

This was a strange conversation. I thought we'd moved past the one-word responses. Then, feeling like an oversensitive idiot, I shifted until my back was against my pillows. I brought my knees up and picked at the fraying edges of my shorts.

"Well, my day has been awful." I closed my eyes as the memory of the day's earlier events rushed through my mind. "Maddie hates me and I'm pretty sure we are going to lose our house to the city."

A lump lodged itself in my throat and I struggled to push it down with a swallow.

Gah. Why couldn't I be stronger? Why was I this emotional basket case?

I waited for Lucas to respond but when he didn't, I glanced down at the screen just to make sure we were still connected. "Lucas?" I asked again, bringing the receiver up to my ear.

"Yeah, I'm here."

I was grateful, yet worried that he hadn't responded. Why was he being so cryptic? Had I done something wrong?

"Everything okay?" I asked.

He sighed. It sounded just as heavy as my own breathing. Then it dawned on me. I knew why he was upset. His dad.

"Winny told me your dad was coming." I winced, not sure if I should say anything or not. But I was tired of keeping everyone else's secrets. I had problems of my own. Didn't people realize this?

Lucas cleared his throat. "You knew about that?" He had hints of hurt in his voice.

Feeling bad, I nodded. "Yeah. I'm sorry I didn't tell you sooner. Winny made me promise not to tell you. I guess she wasn't sure how she felt about it and thought telling you would just bring you down as well."

He was quiet again.

"Can I see you?" I really needed Lucas right now.

"Yeah." His voice was small but I could hear the relief behind his response.

"Come over?"

"Be there in five."

We hung up and I set my phone on my bed as I crossed over to the bathroom. It took some work, but I was able to cover up the lines made from my comforter as well as fix my hair. By the time I got a text from Lucas telling me he was here, I looked less like death.

I pulled open my bedroom door and bounded down the stairs. I needed to see Lucas. I needed to feel his arms around me and his breath in my ear as he told me everything was going to be alright.

I was drowning and the only person who could save me right now was him.

I pulled open the front door and my heart leapt at the sight of his tousled hair and dark, brown eyes. Without thinking, I stepped forward and wrapped my arms around him, burying my face into his neck and taking a deep breath. He smelled like saltwater and sandalwood.

He wrapped his arms around my waist and pulled me closer like I was a life raft and he was drowning. He, too, buried his face in my neck.

I lost track of time, as we stood there wrapped in each other's arms. We weren't speaking but I could feel the stress leave his shoulders as it did mine. This was exactly what I needed.

I needed him.

He pulled back and brushed his lips against mine. "Hey," he whispered, a smile spreading across his lips.

Suddenly, I was nervous. I wasn't sure why, but I suspected it was because I felt so vulnerable and yet, there was nothing I wanted more than to be open and raw with him. "Hey," I whispered.

He smiled and leaned in to press his lips to my forehead. I grabbed his hand and led him over to the porch swing on the far end of the porch where we sat down.

I draped my legs over his and he wrapped his arm around them, drawing them closer to him. He then draped his other arm along the back of the swing and turned to study me.

"Tell me what happened," he said.

I blinked a few times, trying to push the tears away. I'd cried enough for one day, I didn't need to start up again. I took a deep breath and told him everything. From Maddie and our fight, to Dad and the note. I explained how Dad had been keeping the notices a secret, and even when he was confronted with a note from the city telling them this was the last straw, he still dug in his heels, refusing to do anything.

Lucas listened while he traced circles around on the outside of my hand. My body tingled from his touch and in a strange way, it helped calm me down.

By the time I was finished with my story, he'd stopped moving and was just sitting there, holding my hand.

I studied him. What was he thinking?

"I'm sorry, Charlotte," he said, meeting my gaze. I could see the pain in his eyes as he studied me.

"Yeah, I know." I tipped my head back and closed my eyes as the realization of what had happened flooded every part of my body. I shivered in the August heat and then tipped my face forward again and gave him a small smile. Not wanting to dominate the conversation, I asked, "What's the news about your dad?"

Lucas stopped moving and his expression hardened. He dropped his hand as he stared at the boards on the porch. He was quiet and I began to wonder if I had said the wrong thing.

Then I shook my head. "We don't have to talk about it if you don't want to," I hurried. There was no way I wanted to focus on a pain that may be too hard for him to speak.

Lucas sat back and then turned to study me. "It's okay. I can talk about it." He took a deep breath. "He's on his way. I think he"—Lucas glanced at his watch—"He should be landing real soon. Quinn sent me his itinerary."

I nodded to let him know I was listening. "Do you know why he wants to come?"

Lucas stiffened. "Winny says it's to reconnect with me but I have a feeling he knows something."

I raised my eyebrows. That sounded ominous. "About us? Me?"

Lucas met my gaze and I could see an apology forming in his gaze. "I'm sorry. My dad's a prick and I'm not going to let him do anything. It doesn't matter. I can love who I want to."

My lips parted at that tiny, little four letter word. Did he say *love?* Lucas held my gaze as he turned to me.

"I love you, Charlotte." He held my hand and then dipped down to brush his lips across my fingers. "And I won't let my family change that."

I reached up and cradled his cheek with my hand. I wanted to tell him those same words. I wanted to be vulnerable like that. But something was holding me back. A vice around my heart that told me that once those words were spoken, they couldn't be taken back. That allowing myself to care about someone like that would expose myself to a lot of pain.

I loved my mom but that did nothing to save her. She still died, leaving a gaping hole in my chest and a hemorrhaging heart that couldn't be healed.

"I…Lucas…" Tears welled up in my eyes as I attempted to force the same words to leave my lips. But they weren't coming.

He studied me for a moment and then a knowing look passed over his face. "It's okay. I understand." He leaned back and closed his eyes. "When you're ready."

We sat there on the porch swing as silence surrounded us. I closed my eyes and relaxed as Lucas pushed off the ground slightly with his foot, sending the bench to swing.

It wasn't until Lucas' phone rang that we both looked up. I studied Lucas' face as he glanced down at his phone. I knew from that one look who was on the other line.

Mr. Addington.

Lucas swiped his screen and brought the phone to his cheek. "Hey, Dad."

Then he paused. I could hear Mr. Addington talk on the other end. Lucas just listened as he stared off into the distance. He had his arm wrapped around his chest in a protective stance while the other hand held the phone.

Lucas said a few mm hums, and then he hung up.

I studied him, my eyebrows raised.

Lucas finally looked over at me. "I should go. He's going to be at Winny's in ten minutes and he *expects to see me there.*" He dropped his voice a few octaves.

I chewed my lip as I nodded. Suddenly, I didn't want him to go anywhere. I already knew how his dad felt about poor people. Would he feel the same about me? About Lucas and I? Right now, I wasn't sure I could stand losing another important person to me.

As if sensing my worry, Lucas leaned forward and brushed his lips to mine. "Whatever he has to say, it doesn't change how I feel about you," he said, tipping his forehead forward and resting it against mine.

I nodded in acknowledgement even though I knew he couldn't keep that promise. No one could ever stop a train without brakes. I knew the feeling. It never ended well.

He studied my face for a moment longer before he kissed my cheek and stood. He made his way across the deck and just before he bounded down the stairs, he raised his hand. I blew him a kiss and he pretended to catch it in the air.

I giggled as he shoved his hand in his pocket and then descended the steps. Once he was at his car, he pulled open the driver's door and climbed in.

In seconds, I was alone again.

I pulled my feet in tight and hugged my knees as I rested my chin on them. I glanced around, trying to decide what it would feel like if we were forced to leave our house. Where would we go?

My stomach twisted as I thought about starting over in another town. A place where I didn't know everyone and they didn't know me. It sounded lonely and depressing.

This was the house where I'd grown up. Mom died here. This

was the last place I remember her being. If they took this place away, would I even be able to remember her? I needed this house and the connection I felt being here.

I sat there, curled up on the swing until Dad's truck pulled into the driveway and he climbed out beside Drew. Drew was bouncing up and down as he slammed the door, then ran over to grab his football and threw it a few times into the air.

I'd been so wrapped up in my thoughts that I hadn't even noticed that Dad had been gone. Or that Drew had been gone for that matter.

Dad climbed the front steps and paused when his gaze fell on me. His expression was strained as he studied me. His brow was furrowed and I could see the pain in his eyes.

"Where were you?" I asked as I swung my feet to the floor and stood.

Dad fiddled with his keys as he studied them. "The meeting."

The meeting. The meeting where he and the city council decided the fate of our house. Of our future.

I stared at him, waiting for him to answer. When he didn't, I added an exaggerated, "And?"

Dad shrugged as he threw his keys in the air. "It's been decided. We need to get the yard cleared by the weekend or we can no longer stay here."

The world around me slowed from his words. So it was going to happen. "Well? Let's get started." I waved my hands toward the cars and trucks that littered our yard.

Dad's gaze followed my gesture but I could see the hesitation in it. There was no way he wanted this, and he was going to fight me on it. He didn't answer me as he pulled open the front door and walked into the house.

Anger rose up inside of me as I stomped after him. "You can't be serious," I said. My voice was shaky as I tried to contain my feelings.

Dad set his keys in the cup by the door and then slipped off his shoes. "Stop overreacting, Lottie."

Ugh. I hated when he used Mom's nickname like that. Like I was somehow going to forgive him. "Dad, you must be joking."

But, he wasn't listening to me. Instead, he'd walked into the kitchen and pulled out a box of frozen chicken nuggets. Feeling like a pesky fly that was just an annoyance to him, I growled as I fisted my hands.

"Dad!" I couldn't just stand by anymore and let everything fall apart.

Dad hesitated and then slammed the freezer door. "Charlotte, enough," he bellowed. He set the nuggets down on the counter and then rested both hands next to it as he dipped his head down. His shoulders sagged as I watched him take a few deep breaths. "I just can't anymore."

My mouth hung open as I studied him. I wanted to shake him. Wake him up to the reality of the world we were living in. But I couldn't. Not when he wouldn't even listen.

Tired of trying to force him to look up. To acknowledge that our family was falling apart, I grabbed my purse, slung it over my shoulder, and stormed outside.

This was no longer my safe haven and right now. I couldn't figure out my next step in a place I felt so uncertain.

I needed to get out of here. I needed the Bread Basket.

CHAPTER TWENTY

I peddled as fast as I could through the streets of Sweet Water. It almost made me angry to see all the happy people out enjoying the last true day of summer. Fellow students were coming out of the ice cream parlor or throwing Frisbees in the park.

They look so carefree and relaxed.

Not like the pent up, jumble of nerves that I felt. A sob escaped my lips as I skidded to a stop in the back of The Bread Basket. My hands shook as I climbed down and pushed my kickstand into place.

My mind felt foggy as I pulled open the back door and slipped into the cool, air conditioned building.

The smell of yeast and sugar filled my nose—instantly relaxing me. I inhaled a few times and I felt my ragged nerves relaxing. I pulled off my purse and hung it on the hook, then grabbed my apron. I wasn't slotted to work today. In fact, Winny had cut my hours with school looming overhead, but I didn't care and I was pretty sure she didn't either.

She knew how healing baking was to me and right now, I was an open, gushing wound that needed care.

I made my way toward the kitchen, but two deep voices stopped me. Even though I could make out Lucas' tone, something inside of me told me to wait.

I leaned against the wall as my ears perked up.

"I can't believe you've been here a week and it's starting again." The voice was smooth and icy. It sounded like a deeper version of Lucas' so I could only assume that it was his dad.

"This is ridiculous." I heard Lucas sigh in the exaggerated way he did every time he was incredibly annoyed with someone.

"You left me no choice. Your mother is worried about you and so am I. I hope I don't have to remind you what happened to get you sent here in the first place."

Lucas groaned. "Charlotte is not Maggie. She's...different."

There was a pause before Mr. Addington spoke. "Her family is in crisis, did she tell you that?"

My blood ran cold, causing me to shiver. How did he know? I'd only just found out.

"What? How do you know?" Then Lucas paused. "You had Brady check up on her? Seriously?"

"It's in my best interest to find out who my son is dating. I need to know if I should protect my family. My company. Your last little episode caused a 4 percent dip in our stock as well as millions to keep the family quiet." His dad let out a tired sigh. "I'm tired of cleaning up your messes, Lucas."

I chewed my lip as his dad's words settled around me. I was Lucas' mess? I shook my head. What was happening? How could so many things be falling apart so fast?

"Charlotte is not like that. She's different. Something you will never understand. And I love her."

Mr. Addington scoffed. "You do not love her. You don't know what love is. This is infatuation. As soon as you leave, you'll be moving on. Did you tell her that? Your plans after Senior year? How does she feel about your little trip you have planned instead of school?"

My gaze dropped to my fingers as questions formed in my mind. What trip? What was Mr. Addington talking about? And why hadn't Lucas told me?

And then realization dawned on me. Why was I such a fool? Did I really think Lucas and I were going to stay together forever? That he wasn't going to move on? To run away only to finally fall in line and go to college or to run his daddy's company?

And me? Was I that delusional to think that I was a part of any of that?

I swallowed as I tried to force down the pain and anguish that had risen up in my chest, I was a fool to think things were going to last. And if anything, it was better for me to realize that now, when things were still new, than later, when the pain of him leaving would rip my insides apart.

"I'm not following your plan. I thought I already made that pretty clear."

Mr. Addington snorted. "Lucas, you're young. You don't know what you want. And I'm not going to let you throw your future away because you think you understand what consequences mean —where are you going?"

"We're done. You can pack up and head back to your pent-house in New York. I'm not going to sit here and listen to you speak about my life and those I care about."

My heart began to race as Lucas' voice drew closer to me. I wanted to move. I wanted to hide so that he didn't know I was listening to him, but my mind couldn't get my body to work. My feet felt cemented to the ground, and my legs as heavy as bricks.

Suddenly, I was met with the angry gaze of Lucas Addington. His expression morphed into one of confusion as his gaze swept over me.

"Charlotte? What are you doing here?"

I parted my lips to speak, but the words wouldn't come out. How was I supposed to explain this? "I...um..." *Yeah, off to a great start, Charlotte.*

A look of concern flashed over his face as he stepped closer. "Is everything okay? How much did you hear?" He reached out to touch my arm and out of self-preservation, I pulled away from him.

Tears brimmed my eyes as I turned and made my way to the door. I couldn't stay here anymore. The walls felt as if they were closing in on me. Everything was wrong. So very wrong.

"Charlotte," Lucas called as the sound of his footsteps caused my ears to prick.

I was out the door as fast as my feet could carry me. It was such a difference from moments ago when I was standing just outside the kitchen like a statue. Now, the flight response had taken over and I was off.

"Hey!" Lucas' hand surrounded my arm, halting my retreat.

I pulled my arm away, hating how my body reacted to his touch. Every. Single. Time. "Let me go," I murmured as I grabbed my bike handles and climbed onto it, pushing the kickstand out of the way.

He grabbed onto the bar between my handles and dipped down so he could meet my gaze. "Whatever you heard isn't true. My dad's a jerk. I don't care what he thinks." He reached out and cradled my cheek with his hand. "I was supposed to come here. To find you."

A sob escaped my lips as I kept my gaze trained on the dirt in front of me. If I looked at him—if I saw the desperation in his gaze, I'd crack. The dam would break and I wouldn't be able to clean up the mess.

"Stop. Please. We can't," I breathed, finally finding my strength to speak.

He grew quiet and I flicked my gaze over at him for only a moment to see him staring at me.

"You don't mean that," he said. His voice was low and challenging.

I cleared my throat and turned, meeting his gaze head on. "Yes

I do. We were stupid to think we could make this work. You and I come from different worlds." I waved at the air between us.

His jaw flexed as he continued to stare at me. Challenging me. "You don't believe that. You're scared and a coward."

I parted my lips. "I am not a coward."

His knuckles were turning white as he gripped the bar. "Then prove it. Face this fear with me. Be strong. Don't let the uncertainty of the future scare you." He leaned forward with pleading in his gaze. "Tell me you love me."

His words caught me off guard. My breath hitched in my throat as I scrambled to come up with a reason to tell him off. Something that might preserve our friendship while halting the progression of our relationship.

But nothing came to mind. Because the truth was, I wanted him. Body and soul. He was what I was looking for. That life raft while I was drowning. He'd rescued me.

Which was why I needed to back away. I couldn't continue this path if it meant he was leaving. I'd already lost someone I loved, I couldn't do it again.

So, I parted my lips. "I can't say that because it's not true." I pinched my lips shut as I let my reaction linger in the air. Then I wiggled my handlebars. I needed to get out of here before he realized I'd lied. Before I betrayed my resolved and told him the truth.

He stared me down for a moment longer before he pulled his hands away and stepped back. I stifled a sob as I twisted my bike toward the alley as fast as I could. I'm sure I looked like an idiot, but I didn't care. I needed to get out of there and fast.

I pressed my feet down on the pedals and pushed hard—forcing myself to keep my gaze forward. Anything to fight the urge that was building up inside of me to look back. To see if he was watching me. If he wanted me to turn around just as badly as I wanted to turn around.

Did he care?

Once I was on Main street, I took off, reveling in the feeling of my thighs burning as I rode down the street.

I'm not sure how long I biked for, but when I passed the Welcome sign for Jersey, two towns over, and the sun had all but disappeared under the horizon I knew I'd gone far. Needing a break, I rode up to the local gas station where I parked my bike and got off. My legs were wobbly as I straightened and made my way into the cool store.

There were a few people milling around and a middle-aged woman behind the counter. I must have looked like a crazed person, because she straightened, running her gaze over me just to stop at my hair.

"Can I help you, sweetie?"

I shook my head as I followed the sign for restroom. Once I was inside, I shut the door and turned, a yelp escaping my lips.

My hair was wind blown and ratty. My eyes were swollen and my cheeks tear stained. Whatever makeup I'd been wearing was now sliding down my face from sweat and exhaustion.

I reached up and ran my fingers through my hair, wincing as they caught every knot and tangle there. I should have documented this. I'm sure I would have won some sort of Guiness World Record for nastiest hair.

After I splashed some water on my face and dried with the hand dryer, I threw my hair up into a messy bun and felt ten times better.

I unlocked the bathroom door and pulled on it, stepping out into the hallway only to run into a beefy trucker. I apologized under my breath as I slipped past him and into the store. I bought and subsequently devoured five hot dogs outside while I slurped a slushy. By the time I was done, I was stuffed and I didn't feel any better than I had when I walked into the gas station.

I crumpled up the wrappers and threw them into the garbage behind me. Glancing at my watch, I realized I had been gone for a few hours now. I was sure Dad was worried about me. And even though I was mad at him, I didn't like it when he worried. We'd gone through enough to know when to call each other. The last thing I wanted was for him to think I was dead in a ditch somewhere.

After I shot him a quick text, I pulled my purse strap higher onto my shoulder and made my way over to my bike only to discover that my front tire was flat.

I cursed under my breath as I bent down to study it. I pressed on the limp rubber and sighed. Well, that sucked. What was I going to do now?

There really wasn't anyone I wanted to call at this moment. I was mad at anyone who cared enough to come get me. I shook my head as thoughts of Mom entered my mind. I wished she were alive every other minute of my life but right now, I wished it so hard I thought I was going to burst.

She'd know what to do about Dad. She'd tell me what to do about Maddie and Lucas and Mr. Addington. She'd bring me to the tiny doughnut shop we discovered during one of our walks, buy me a giant cherry filled long john, and would tell me everything would be okay as she wiped the cherry innards from my face.

And I'd believe her no matter how insurmountable the challenge felt.

I wiped at my cheeks, grateful that I'd cried just about all my tears earlier. I fiddled with my purse strap as I glanced around. There was one person I could call who I wasn't mad at.

She was the one person who wouldn't judge me.

Winny.

CHAPTER TWENTY-ONE

I waited, leaning against the outside of the gas station for Winny. She had seemed a tad confused about where I was but after I explained, she said she'd be there as fast as she could.

That call had been about a half an hour ago, which meant she should be here any minute. Two bright headlights blinded me as Winny's familiar car pulled into the parking lot. I pushed off the wall and made my way over to the passenger door.

My heart soared when I saw her familiar smile and twinkling eyes. She looked so relaxed and just what I needed when I felt as horrible as I did.

"Pop the trunk so I can stuff my bike into it," I said, waving toward the back.

She nodded and the familiar popping sound of a latch releasing filled the air. I grabbed my bike and wheeled it to the back. After some finagling with the back seats, I was able to shove the bike into the back and slam the trunk. I was pretty sure it wouldn't pop open, but I tapped a few times for good measure.

Then I climbed into the passenger seat and buckled.

Enya was playing softly from the speakers as Winny put the

car in reverse and backed out and onto the highway that connected the towns.

We rode in silence for a few minutes until Winny glanced over at me.

"So, are you going to tell me what your joy ride was about?"

I glanced over at her and laughed. "A joy ride is something you do when the vehicle was stolen," I corrected her.

She went quiet for a minute before she said, "That's what that means? I always thought it just meant an enjoyable ride."

I shook my head. "Nope. And yes, well, sort of."

She wrinkled her nose like she wasn't following my train of thought.

"What I meant to say was that I sort of enjoyed my bike ride. I had—I needed to work off some stress."

Her expression softened as she glanced over at me. "I heard."

The lump returned to my throat. I was getting so used to that lump that I almost pulled up a chair for it and welcomed it to stay for a bit. I couldn't remember a time when I wasn't close to tears.

"What part?"

Winny tapped her fingers on the steering wheel. "Lucas. Keith. Your dad."

I felt her gaze on me. Not able to meet it, I studied my hands that were clasped in my lap. "Yeah. Not the best day in a long shot."

She reached out and patted my hands. "Why don't you tell me what happened. I want to hear it from your lips."

I leaned back in my seat and sighed. It really wasn't what I wanted to do, but what other choice did I have? Besides, maybe it would help me to say the words out loud. To work through the confusion that was plaguing my mind.

I fell into a rhythm of talking and listening to Winny when she gave advice. Which, it turns out, she was a master at. By the time she pulled into my driveway, she turned to face me head on, her arm draped over the steering wheel.

"I think it's best to just let some things lie right now. With your dad and the city. With Lucas." Her gaze intensified at his name, like I needed that extra help in that department.

I fiddled with my purse as I stared down at it. As much as it hurt, she was right. So much had happened in such a small amount of time that it was probably best to let things lie. At least until I figured out how I felt about everything.

It hurt, the fact that I was slowly losing the people in my life. I'd never felt this alone since Mom's funeral and it wasn't something that I cared for. But it wasn't like there was anything else I could do. Lucas and I would never work. Dad was in La-La land right now, and Maddie? Well, I needed to give her a few days to cool down.

I was semi-confident that with enough time, she'd find it in her heart to forgive me. And if not, I'd reach out to her. I mean, we would always be friends. There was no way we could allow a guy to change that.

I leaned over and gave Winny a quick hug. She returned it while wishing me a good first day of Senior year. I nodded as I pulled on the door handle and stepped out of her car. After retrieving my bike, I pushed it up to the garage and then turned and smiled as Winny backed out onto the road.

Now alone, I made my way up the porch steps to the front door. The house was quiet when I walked inside. I peeked around the corners only to find that Dad and Drew weren't around. I took a deep breath as exhaustion filled my muscles.

Sleep was the only thing that could calm my mind right now.

I dragged myself upstairs and quickly dressed into my pajamas. I dive bombed my bed and scooted until I'd pulled the covers up to my chin. I hugged the stuffed animal that Mom bought me when I was five and had the chicken pox. It was ratty and old, but it was one of the only things I had that reminded me of Mom and right now, I needed her next to me.

I closed my eyes and soon, darkness took over as my muscles relaxed and I slipped into unconsciousness.

———

"Get up!" Drew's voice ripped through my dreams, causing me to jump and lift my arms to protect myself.

I harrumphed as he landed directly on my body. I groaned as I flipped to my back and wrapped my arms around my little brother.

"I don't remember asking for a wake-up call," I said, still groggy from sleep.

Drew was bright eyed as he stared up at me. "Dad said we can't be late on our first day and that I should come wake you up." He shrugged and then wiggled, trying to free himself from my clutches. I let out a maniacal laugh and pinned him with one arm and wiggled my fingers into his armpit with the other.

He let out a squeal as he wrenched his body to free himself.

"We need to teach you how to wake people up nicely," I said as I leaned down and shoved my face close to his.

He furrowed his brow and shrugged. "I like jumping on you."

I sighed as I let go of him—after which he instantly sprang up and started jumping on my bed—and leaned back on my headboard.

"Drew," I complained as he narrowly missed jumping on my ankle.

Drew didn't change his rhythm so I pulled my legs up to protect myself. Then he stilled and got a confused look on his face.

"Are we going to have to move?" He peered over at me with his eyes wide.

Worry crept up in my stomach as I reached up and pulled him down so I could give him a squeeze. "Why do you say that?"

"What does seizure mean?"

Oh man, he'd seen the sign. How was I supposed to talk to him about this? It wasn't my job, it was Dad's. He needed to be the one to take ownership of what would happen to our family and our home if he didn't figure his crap out.

"The city just isn't happy that Dad has so many cars out front. We need to clean it up or we'll have to move."

Drew grew quiet and when I glanced down, I could see him studying my comforter as he tried to process my words. "Where would we go? Somewhere it snows?" He whipped around and stared at me with big, hopeful eyes.

I squeezed him and chuckled. Leave it to Drew to find the joy in the misery. "I don't know, bud. Maybe."

Drew wiggled from my grasp and slipped off my bed. "That sounds cool," he said as he sprinted from my room.

Now alone, I glanced over at the clock. Crap. I had fifteen minutes to shower, dress, and be on my way to school—wait. I had no bike which meant, I only had five minutes to get ready.

I threw off my covers and sprinted into the bathroom. After running a brush through my hair and throwing on a floral summer dress, I grabbed my backpack that was full of all my first-day of school needs, and headed downstairs.

Dad was sitting at the table, staring at a bunch of papers. I tried not to glare at him as I passed by, heading toward the kitchen where I grabbed an apple and granola bar from the counter.

"I'm going to be late," I said when I saw Dad turn to talk to me.

He raised an eyebrow and nodded. It was nice that he wasn't going to push me today. I was grateful that he realized that perhaps, I needed some time.

"Oh, okay. Well, have a great first day, sweetie."

I just nodded as guilt rose up inside of my stomach. I knew I shouldn't be mad at Dad. He was just trying to do his best—even if his best meant getting kicked out of our house. I needed to be patient with him, but that was hard to do when our home was on the line.

I bit into the apple as I slipped on my sandals and headed out the back door. The warm morning air greeted me as I pulled my backpack straps up onto my shoulders and hooked my thumb through one side. I kept my gaze down as I stared at the gravel and started the ten-minute walk to school.

I allowed my thoughts to wander as I continued, munching on my apple until it was nothing but a core. I wasn't sure what I was thinking about. To be honest, there was so much I needed to process that I wasn't sure where to even start.

It was probably best to not think about anything at all.

I was doing a pretty good job of that when the sound of a horn honking caused me to jump and my heart to pound. I turned to see Winny's car behind me. Lucas was in the driver's seat, staring at me.

I swallowed, forcing my body to calm, which felt futile. There was no way I was ever going to feel the same in Lucas' presence. Too much had changed. For good and bad.

Not knowing what to do, I just waved at him as I moved farther onto the grass next to me. From the corner of my eye, I saw his brow furrow and suddenly, he was moving. The driver's door opened and he hopped onto the road.

I avoided looking at him as I moved down the street. I didn't want to talk to him. What was he doing? Hadn't I made it clear that there was no way we could ever make it work? We were destined to fail.

Suddenly, his hand surrounded my elbow and he pulled tight so I couldn't move. I hesitated, but refused to look at him.

"You're not talking to me anymore?"

My stomach squeezed as I picked out the hurt and pain that coated his tone. He was hurting just as bad as I was.

"Lucas, I don't think this is a good idea." I couldn't be with him. Why couldn't he just accept that?

"But, Charlotte—"

I held up my hand to stop him. I couldn't do this. It was a struggle to be strong with him gone, it was worse when he was around. "Please, just let me go." I braved heartbreak and lifted my eyes to meet his.

Big mistake.

His brow was furrowed and there was so much anguish in his eyes that it took my breath away. I could see the confusion and hurt written all over his face.

He studied me for a moment as if he were trying to figure out if what I was saying was true. I forced every relaxed and calm feeling to the surface so he couldn't see the real truth. That I was dying inside.

"I can't," he mumbled as he shoved his hands through his hair.

I swallowed as a lump formed in my throat. "Yes, you can. You'll be fine without me."

He shoved his hands into his front pockets as he flicked his gaze away and then back to me. He squinted and I could tell he wanted to say something, but wasn't sure how.

Not wanting to stand here in pain any longer, I gave him a small smile and waved in the direction of school. "I've gotta go. I'm going to be late if I stay here any longer."

He glanced in the direction I motioned and then back to me. "Where's your bike?"

I sighed. "Flat tire."

He pinched his lips together and nodded. I prayed that he wouldn't ask me if he could give me a ride. And just my luck, he didn't. Instead, when he parted his lips he said, "My dad's a fool. He doesn't understand what I want but that doesn't mean I'm going to stop fighting. He'll come around. I'm sure of it."

He was still fighting for me. Why? I'd given him an out. Told him it was okay to break things off. That he didn't need to feel sorry for me anymore.

Not sure how to answer him. I just closed my lips and nodded.

Then I grabbed onto my backpack and turned, making my way to school. His words swarmed in my mind as I tried to ignore the fact that I still hadn't heard him leave.

"I'm going to fight for you, Charlotte Robinson. I won't leave you no matter how hard you push me away."

A sob escaped my lips as his words surrounded me. I hated how he could make my heart sing with just one gesture. I wanted to turn around and tell him he was a fool. But I couldn't. Instead, I just angrily wiped my tears and ducked my head down as I quickened my pace.

I couldn't get my hopes up no matter how much every part of my being wanted me to.

CHAPTER TWENTY-TWO

$\mathcal{T}$he first week of school flew by. I did everything I could think of to keep myself busy. I was up and out of the house before Dad and Drew were up and I stayed at school, volunteering to help teachers until dinnertime. Then I'd rush home, grab whatever plate of food Dad made up for me that night, and hid out in my room claiming too much homework.

It was exhausting but it kept me distracted.

Lucas tried to approach me a few times in the halls, but I successfully dodged him. Either running into the bathroom or walking backwards to take a different hall.

Maddie was cold at first, but we had art and communications together and by the end of the week, she was at least smiling at me. I felt hopeful that I might be able to fix things.

The final bell rang Friday afternoon and I slipped out of my desk in Calc. and grabbed my backpack. I scanned the hall when I got to the door and when I didn't see Lucas, I stepped out and headed toward my locker.

Maddie was waiting there with a grin on her face. Relief flooded my body when I saw her. Maybe this awful nightmare would be over. I needed my best friend now more than ever, especially since tomorrow was the last day we had to clean up our yard or the city would take over. And nothing had been moved.

"Hey," I said. I kept my voice quiet even though I was celebrating inside. I didn't want to scare her off.

She wrapped both arms around me and pulled me into a hug. "Hey," she said. Then she pulled back to study me. "I'm so sorry," she whispered.

A tear rolled down my cheek but all I could do was nod. "Me, too."

She grinned at me and I could see the tears brimming her lids as well. "I was a jealous idiot." I pinched my lips together, fighting a nod. She laughed as she waved her hand at me. "You can acknowledge that."

I giggled as I lowered my backpack to the floor and started dialing my combination. "Yeah, you kind of were."

She gasped but when I glanced over at her, I could see her playful smile. Well, this was going to be fun.

"Wanna hear something amazing?"

I pulled open my locker and began shuffling my books around. "Always."

"Liam Johnson is in my Chem. class."

When she didn't continue, I glanced over at her. There had to be more to this story than she was letting on. She had her lips pinched shut as if she were waiting for me to react.

"And?" I asked, drawing out every syllable.

"And…he invited me to his house on Sunday." She wiggled her eyebrows.

I nodded as a smile emerged on my lips. That sounded like Maddie. It was good to see that she'd moved past Lucas. And then, just thinking his name caused my chest to squeeze. I should be a tad angry that she'd moved on so quickly when she made me feel so horrible for liking him, but it wouldn't have mattered. Lucas and I weren't meant for each other.

I must have been quiet for too long because suddenly, she was in my line of sight, studying me. Her expression softened as she reached out and touched my arm. "I'm sorry, Char."

I forced a smile and turned back to my locker, grateful for the distraction. "It's okay," I muttered as I finished shoving a notebook into my backpack.

"I was a jerk. A jealous jerk. And you didn't deserve that."

I nodded. It was true. She'd been a crappy friend but I'd been one as well. I glanced over at her and shrugged. "It's okay. It wasn't meant to be anyway. I mean, you saved me from making a mistake and getting in involved deeper than was wise." I shook my head as my response was processed in my mind. What the heck was I saying? It was like gibberish.

Maddie got a glint to her eyes that had me studying her. Why did she look so cryptic? Too tired to figure things out, I sighed and slammed my locker shut and shouldered my backpack. "Wanna hang out tomorrow? I could use a milkshake and movie."

Maddie pinched her lips together and shook her head. "I can't. I've got something else going on."

Great. First day with nothing to do and my best friend couldn't save me. Instead, I was forced to stay at home where I was going to hide out in my room to avoid Dad.

She gave me a squeeze and pulled away. "You'll be fine. And who knows, maybe things will start looking up," she said in a cryptic tone as she waved at me and headed toward the exit.

I stared at her retreating frame with my forehead creased and confusion on my face.

What did that mean?

———

I woke up Saturday morning to the sound of beeping. I peeled open my eyes and stared at the ceiling as I focused in on the sound.

Was I imagining things?

I sat up and glanced around. Nope. It sounded like a truck backing up.

I pulled off the covers and padded over to my window, my jaw dropping when I saw three large semi trucks parked alongside our house. Each was trailing a large flatbed behind it.

Another truck was carrying a backhoe that was currently being backed off the bed and onto the ground. I grabbed the nearest clothes and dressed. Then I pounded down the stairs and into the living room.

Dad was standing in front of the bay window, watching what was happening.

"You did it?" I asked, my voice all high and squeaky.

Dad turned to study me. "No," he said. His voice was quiet. "Well, I tried, but..." His voice trailed off as a look of shame crossed his face.

Not wanting to have secrets anymore, I reached out and grabbed his arms. "What's going on?"

He glanced up at me, his eyes filling with tears. "I wanted to fix this. I did. But it was going to cost too much money. The only way we could afford it was if I used the money your mom had set aside for you and Drew." He swallowed, causing his Adam's apple to bob up and down. "I couldn't do that."

So that's what this had all been about? Dad not wanting to use something Mom left us? "Dad, that's crazy. If you have the money, fix it."

He pulled away from my hands as he scrubbed his face. "I couldn't do that. You'd already lost so much and I couldn't let my stupidity take one more thing from you two."

I chewed my lip as I stared at my dad. A man who had always been strong, seemed so broken right now.

"So then, we're losing the house?" Worry filled my stomach as I turned to stare out the window. But then, as I studied the people walking around my yard, I realized, I recognized them.

There was Pastor Bryant and his wife. There was Maddie and her parents. Even Winny was walking around gathering up scrap metal and bringing it over to a dump truck.

"Dad?" I yelled out but then I glanced over and saw him a few inches away from me. "What's going on?"

He glanced over at me, and then back out the window. "I don't know."

Completely confused, I made my way over to the front door and opened it. I stepped out onto the porch and glanced around. When I saw Maddie, I hurried down the stairs and over to her.

"What the—what are you doing here?"

She glanced over at me with a huge smile on her face. "Surprise!" she exclaimed.

I stared at her, not processing what was going on. "Surprise?"

She giggled and reached down to pick up a discarded bumper. "I think the person you need to ask is over there." She waved behind me.

Turning, my mouth dropped open. Lucas was standing right next to one of the truck's cabs, talking to a beefy guy with a hard hat on. My whole body went numb as I turned to Maddie. "What's he doing here?"

She studied me and then her expression turned serious. "You need to go talk to him."

I closed my eyes and shook my head. "I can't. No. I can't."

She grabbed onto my shoulders, pulling me back to the present. "You have to, Char."

I swallowed as I peeked at her. "But, I was so mean. And his dad hates me so much…" My voice cracked as the things that I said to him raced into my mind. I'd been horrible to him. Why would he ever want to talk to me?

"I'm thinking he doesn't care," Maddie said.

I turned to her. "What? Why?"

She pinched her lips together and then sighed. "Fine. But he made everyone promise they wouldn't say…he arranged this whole thing. He got a lot of businesses to donate money to help your dad out. Not only with cleaning up, but renting a few acres outside of town so he can keep his cars." She raised her eyebrows as if she were anticipating my response.

I didn't realize it, but I was staring at Lucas while listening to Maddie. I had heard the words she'd said, but they didn't seem to be registering. "He, what?"

As if sensing that he was being talked about, he turned and met my gaze. Too embarrassed, I dropped my attention to the ground and stared at the patch of grass at my feet.

"I've got to..." Maddie's voice trailed off as she moved away. I wanted to reach out and grab her and demand that she stayed next to me, but when I saw the tips of Lucas' shoes, I knew why she'd left.

"Hey."

I closed my eyes as the familiarity of Lucas' voice washed over me. I swallowed as pain and anger at myself and the situation we were now in washed over me. I wanted to acknowledge him. I wanted to tell him I was sorry, but my body was resisting. It was like I was stuck and I couldn't remember how to talk.

Lucas cleared his throat, which startled me. I glanced up to see him studying me. There was an earnestness to his gaze that both pulled me in and scared me to death. Not sure what I should do, I parted my lips just as panic coursed through my body.

Instead of standing there, having a panic attack in front of him, I clamped my lips shut and turned, running/walking the heck out of there.

I didn't stop until I was inside and shutting the door behind me. Once I was alone, I leaned against the wall and buried my face in my hands. What was Lucas doing? Why was he so insistent on being nice to me?

I didn't deserve it.

I didn't deserve any of this.

I was the one who ran. I was the one who broke this off. He deserved someone better than me. Someone who could make him happy and not run at the first sign of trouble. I was the last person he should get involved with.

"Charlotte."

I yelped as Lucas' soft voice startled me. I turned to see him standing a few feet off. His gaze was hesitant and his hands were shoved into his front pockets.

Tears welled up in my eyes as I dropped my gaze and turned so he couldn't see me. I was too ashamed for how I had reacted. How I had treated him from the moment we met.

"I'm...you..." I took a deep breath as nothing I wanted to say came out right. I was tripping over myself like the idiot I was.

His eyebrows rose as he studied me. I could see him from the corner of my eye. There was a look of sympathy on his face. Which only made me feel worse. I didn't want to be a project for him. I didn't want him to think that I was this unhinged girl who was going to snap at any minute.

I held my breath for a moment to gather my courage and then turned. No more running. No more hiding. I was going to face the thing that terrified me the most. I could be strong. I was tired of feeling so weak.

"I'm sorry," tumbled out before I could stop myself.

Lucas looked confused as he studied my face. "For what?"

I chewed my lip as emotions rose up in my chest. What was I sorry for? Everything possible answer felt too trite. There was a lot I was sorry for, but the biggest one was the scariest. One of the largest lies I'd ever told anyone.

"For saying I didn't love you." The words left my lips in a whisper.

Lucas leaned forward as if trying to catch what I'd said. When he returned his gaze to my face, his expression had morphed into one of unbelief. "What?"

I took another deep breath and forced my courage as I said, "For saying I didn't love you." This time, about ten decibels louder than before.

Lucas snapped back as he stared at me. "You love me?"

A tear escaped my lashes. "Yes."

He ran his hands through his hair. His gaze roamed the room before returning to my face. "You. Love me." He pointed to my chest and then back to himself.

That's what I thought I'd said. Maybe I'd been wrong "I—"

Lucas closed the gap, wrapping his arms around my waist and pulling me up to him. He pressed his lips to mine in a hungry and desperate way. I was startled for only a minute but then realization dawned and I discovered that this was the only place I really wanted to be. Wrapped up in Lucas' arms.

He was everything I wanted and yet didn't know I needed. He challenged me and completed me in this strange, cosmic way.

I wrapped my hands around the nape of his neck and pulled him closer. There was no way I was going to let him go this time.

He left me breathless when he pulled away. I wanted to protest. To command him to never stop kissing me. But, from the earnest look in his eyes, I could tell he needed to say something.

"This last week has been complete torture. I've never felt so alone in my life." He pressed his lips to my forehead.

"I'm sorry," I whispered, leaning back so he could feel the weight of my apology.

He shook his head. "Don't be. You weren't wrong. My family... my dad. I come from a place where your life is planned out for you and I can't say it's going to be easy. They will continue to voice their displeasure." He gently kissed my cheeks and the tip of my nose. "But I promise, no matter what, I will never leave. You're stuck with me for a very long time."

I swallowed as fear of the unknown crept up inside of my chest. I wanted to believe him—no, *needed* to. It was just my lack of confidence spilling over.

As if sensing my worry, he pulled me close and gently kissed my lips. Tingles erupted across my skin from the intensity of it. It was like he was reassuring me.

"I will prove myself to you if you let me try," he said when he broke away. His voice was deep and emotion filled.

His words and meaning washed over me, burying any fear or doubt that lingered.

"Promise?" I asked. I didn't need him to answer. I already knew what he was going to say. And I already knew what I was going to do. Despite my fear, I was going to love Lucas for a very long time.

"Promise," he said, finding my pinkie and entwining it with his.

I reached up my free hand and cradled his cheek with it. Then I rose up onto my toes and kissed him again. This time, with as much feeling as I could muster.

There was a knock on the window, pulling Lucas and me apart. I glanced over to see Dad standing there with a strangely protective look on his face.

"You two about done?" he asked.

I giggled as I glanced over at Lucas.

"Yep, Mr. Robinson. We're coming."

Lucas pulled open the door and I followed him out onto the porch. We stood there, surveying the work being done. Everyone seemed in good spirits and for the first time since I could remember, I could see grass instead of hunks of metal.

I wrapped my arms around Lucas' waist and laid my head against his chest. "How did you do this?"

He pressed his lips to the top of my head. "This town loves your family. Everyone wanted to help. That's the beauty of this place."

I forced a shocked expression as I tipped back to stare at him. "Is Lucas Addington falling in love with Sweet Water?"

He let out a pfsst sound but then his expression softened.

"Maybe. It was easy when I found a fabulous girl who opened my eyes up to all it had to offer."

I smiled, the feeling of complete satisfaction rising up from my toes and exploding in my chest.

We held each other for a moment longer before Dad yelled at us to get to work. I giggled as we descended the steps, holding each other's hands until the last minute. Then, we parted, going to different ends of the yard to help clean up.

It had been a long time since I'd felt this loved, felt this complete and even though there were still a lot of unknowns, I knew, that with the people around me, I was going to be just fine.

I tipped my gaze toward the sky and smiled.

"Thanks for looking out for me, Mom," I whispered. "I think we're going to be okay."

And I meant it. Every single word.

***

Join Anne-Marie's Newsletter!
Find great deals on my books and other sweet romance!
Get, Fighting Love for the Cowboy FREE
just for signing up!
Grab it HERE!

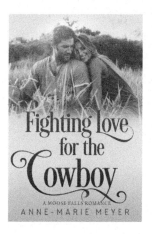

She's an IRS auditor desperate to prove herself.
He's a cowboy trying to hold onto his ranch.
Love was not on the agenda.

OTHER BOOKS BY ANNE-MARIE MEYER

CLEAN ADULT ROMANCES

Forgetting the Billionaire

Book 1 of the Clean Billionaire Romance series

Forgiving the Billionaire

Book 2 of the Clean Billionaire Romance series

Finding Love with the Billionaire

Book 3 of the Clean Billionaire Romance series

Falling for the Billionaire

Book 4 of the Clean Billionaire Romance series

Fixing the Billionaire

Book 5 of the Clean Billionaire Romance series

The Complete Billionaire Series

The Whole Series for $9.99

Marrying a Cowboy

Book 1 of a Fake Marriage series

Fighting Love for the Cowboy

Book 1 of A Moose Falls Romance

Marrying an Athlete

Book 2 of a Fake Marriage series

Marrying a Billionaire

Book 3 of a Fake Marriage series

Marrying a Prince

Book 4 of a Fake Marriage series

Marrying a Spy

Book 5 of a Fake Marriage series

Second Chance Mistletoe Kisses

Book 1 of Love Tries Again series

CLEAN YA ROMANCES

Rule #1: You Can't Date the Coach's Daughter

Book 1 of the Rules of Love series

Rule #2: You Can't Crush on Your Sworn Enemy

Book 2 of the Rules of Love series

Rule #3: You Can't Kiss Your Best Friend

Book 3 of the Rules of Love series

Rule #4: You Can't Misinterpret a Mistletoe Kiss

Book 4 of the Rules of Love series

My Christmas Break Mistake

Book 1 of The Best Mistakes Series

ABOUT THE AUTHOR

Anne-Marie Meyer lives in MN with her husband, four boys, and baby girl. She loves romantic movies and believes that there is a FRIENDS quote for just about every aspect of life.

Connect with Anne-Marie on these platforms!
anne-mariemeyer.com

f

Made in the USA
Coppell, TX
23 November 2020